PENGUIN BOOKS

TRISTESSA

Jack Kerouac was born in Lowell, Massachusetts, in 1922, the youngest of three children in a Franco-American family. He attended local Catholic and public schools and won a football scholarship to Columbia University in New York City, where he first met Neal Cassady, Allen Ginsberg, and William S. Burroughs. He quit school in his sophomore year after a dispute with his football coach, and joined the Merchant Marine, beginning the restless wanderings that were to continue for the greater part of his life. His first novel, *The Town and the City*, appeared in 1950, but it was *On the Road*, first published in 1957 and memorializing his adventures with Neal Cassady, that epitomized to the world what became known as "the Beat generation" and made Kerouac one of the most controversial and best-known writers of his time. Publication of his many other books followed, among them *The Dharma Bums, The Subterraneans*, and *Big Sur*. Kerouac considered them all to be part of *The Duluoz Legend*. "In my old age," he wrote, "I intend to collect all my work and reinsert my pantheon of uniform names, leave the long shelf full of books there, and die happy." He died in St. Petersburg, Florida, in 1969, at the age of forty-seven.

By Jack Kerouac

The Town and the City
The Scripture of the Golden Eternity
Some of the Dharma
Old Angel Midnight
Good Blonde and Others
Pull My Daisy
Trip Trap
Pic
The Portable Jack Kerouac
Selected Letters: 1940–1956
Selected Letters: 1957–1969
Atop an Underwood
Orpheus Emerged

POETRY
Mexico City Blues
Scattered Poems
Pomes All Sizes
Heaven and Other Poems
Book of Blues
Book of Haikus

THE DULUOZ LEGEND
Visions of Gerard
Doctor Sax
Maggie Cassidy
Vanity of Duluoz
On the Road
Visions of Cody
The Subterraneans
Tristessa
Lonesome Traveller
Desolation Angels
The Dharma Bums
Book of Dreams
Big Sur
Satori in Paris

TRISTESSA

Jack Kerouac

PENGUIN BOOKS

PENGUIN BOOKS
Published by the Penguin Group
Penguin Group (USA) Inc., 375 Hudson Street, New York, New York 10014, U.S.A.
Penguin Group (Canada), 90 Eglinton Avenue East, Suite 700, Toronto, Ontario,
Canada M4P 2Y3 (a division of Pearson Penguin Canada Inc.)
Penguin Books Ltd, 80 Strand, London WC2R 0RL, England
Penguin Ireland, 25 St Stephen's Green, Dublin 2, Ireland
(a division of Penguin Books Ltd)
Penguin Group (Australia), 250 Camberwell Road, Camberwell, Victoria 3124,
Australia (a division of Pearson Australia Group Pty Ltd)
Penguin Books India Pvt Ltd, 11 Community Centre, Panchsheel Park,
New Delhi – 110 017, India
Penguin Group (NZ), 67 Apollo Drive, Rosedale, North Shore 0632, New Zealand
(a division of Pearson New Zealand Ltd)
Penguin Books (South Africa) (Pty) Ltd, 24 Sturdee Avenue,
Rosebank, Johannesburg 2196, South Africa

Penguin Books Ltd, Registered Offices: 80 Strand, London WC2R 0RL, England

First published in the United States of America by
Avon Books 1960
Published in Penguin Books 1992

30 29

PUBLISHER'S NOTE
This is a work of fiction. Names, characters, places, and incidents either
are the product of the author's imagination or are used fictitiously, and
any resemblance to actual persons, living or dead, events, or locales is
entirely coincidental.

LIBRARY OF CONGRESS CATALOGING IN PUBLICATION DATA
Kerouac, Jack, 1922–1969.
Tristessa/Jack Kerouac.
p. cm.
ISBN 978-0-14-016811-2
I. Title.
PS3521.E735T73   1992
813'.54—dc20   91–43531

Printed in the United States of America

PART ONE

Trembling and Chaste

I'M RIDING ALONG with Tristessa in the cab, drunk, with big bottle of Juarez Bourbon whiskey in the till-bag railroad lootbag they'd accused me of holding in railroad 1952—here I am in Mexico City, rainy Saturday night, mysteries, old dream sidestreets with no names reeling in, the little street where I'd walked through crowds of gloomy Hobo Indians wrapped in tragic shawls enough to make you cry and you thought you saw knives flashing beneath the folds—lugubrious dreams as tragic as the one of Old Railroad Night where my father sits big of thighs in smoking car of night, outside's a brakeman with red light and white light, lumbering in the sad vast mist tracks of life—but now I'm up on that Vegetable plateau Mexico, the moon of Citlapol a few nights earlier I'd stumbled to on the sleepy roof on the way to the ancient dripping stone toilet—Tristessa is high, beautiful as ever, goin home gayly to go to bed and enjoy her morphine.

Night before I've in a quiet hassel in the rain sat with her darkly at Midnight counters eating bread and soup and drinking Delaware Punch, and I'd come out of that interview with a vision of Tristessa in my bed in my arms, the strangeness of her love-cheek, Azteca, Indian girl with mysterious lidded Billy Holliday eyes and spoke with great melancholic voice like Luise Rainer sadfaced Viennese actresses that made all Ukraine cry in 1910.

Gorgeous ripples of pear shape her skin to her cheekbones, and long sad eyelids, and Virgin Mary resignation, and peachy coffee complexion and eyes of astonishing mystery with nothing-but-earth-depth expressionless half disdain and half mournful lamentation of pain. "I am seek," she's always saying to me and Bull at the pad—I'm in Mexico City wildhaired and mad riding in a cab down past the Ciné Mexico in rainy traffic jams, I'm swigging from the bottle, Tristessa is trying long harangues to explain that the night before when I put her in the cab the driver'd tried to make her and she hit him with her fist, news which the present driver receives without comment—We're going down to Tristessa's house to sit and get high—Tristessa has warned me that the house will be a mess because her sister is drunk and sick, and El Indio will be there standing majestically with morphine needle downward in the big brown arm, glitter-eyed looking right at you or expecting the prick of the needle to bring the wanted flame itself and going "Hm-za . . . the Aztec needle in my flesh of flame" looking all a whole lot like the big cat in Culiao

who presented me the 0 the time I came down to Mexico
to see other visions—My whiskey bottle has strange Mexican soft covercap that I keep worrying will slip off and
all my bag be drowned in Bourbon 86 proof whiskey.

Through the crazy Saturday night drizzle streets like
Hong Kong our cab pushes slowly through the Market
ways and we come out on the whore street district and
get off behind the fruity fruitstands and tortilla beans
and tacos shacks with fixed wood benches—It's the poor
district of Rome.

I pay the cab 3.33 by giving cabbie 10 pesos and asking
"seis" for change, which I get without comment and
wonder if Tristessa thinks I am too splurgy like big John
Drunk in Mexico—But no time to think, we are hurrying
through the slicky sidewalks of glisten-neon reflections
and candle lights of little sidewalk sitters with walnuts
on a towel for sale—turn quickly at the stinky alleyway
of her tenement cell-house one story high—We go
through dripping faucets and pails and boys and duck
under wash and come to her iron door, which from
adobe withins is unlocked and we step in the kitchen the
rain still falling from the leaves and boards that served
as the kitchen roof—allowing little drizzles to fizzle in
the kitchen over the chicken garbage in the damp corner—Where, miraculously, now, I see the little pink cat
taking a little pee on piles of okra and chickenfeed—
The inside bedroom is littered completely and ransacked
as by madmen with torn newspapers and the chicken's
pecking at the rice and the bits of sandwiches on the

floor—On the bed lay Tristessa's "sister" sick, wrapped in pink coverlet—it's as tragic as the night Eddy was shot on the rainy Russia Street—

TRISTESSA IS SITTING on the edge of the bed adjusting her nylon stockings, she pulls them awkwardly from her shoes with big sad face overlooking her endeavors with pursy lips, I watch the way she twists her feet inward convulsively when she looks at her shoes.

She is such a beautiful girl, I wonder what all my friends would say back in New York and up in San Francisco, and what would happen down in Nola when you see her cutting down Canal Street in the hot sun and she has dark glasses and a lazy walk and keeps trying to tie her kimono to her thin overcoat as though the kimono was supposed to tie to the coat, tugging convulsively at it and goofing in the street saying "Here ees the cab—hey hees hey who—there you go—I breeng you back the m o a - n y." Money's moany. She makes money sound like my old French Canadian Aunt in Lawrence "It's not you moany, that I want, it's you l o a v e"—Love is loave. "Eets you l a w v." The law is lawv.—Same with Tristessa, she is so high all the time, and sick, shooting ten gramos of morphine per month,—staggering down the city streets yet so beautiful people keep turning and looking at her—Her eyes are radiant and shining and her cheek is wet from the mist and her Indian hair is black and cool and slick hangin in 2 pigtails behind with the roll-sod hairdo behind (the correct Cathedral Indian hairdo)—Her shoes she keeps looking at are brand new not scrawny, but she lets her nylons keep falling and keeps pulling on them and convulsively twisting her feet—You picture what a beautiful girl in New York, wearing a flowery wide skirt a la New Look with Dior flat bosomed pink cashmere sweater, and her lips and eyes do the same and do the rest. Here she is reduced to impoverished Indian Lady gloomclothes—You see the Indian ladies in the inscrutable dark of doorways, look-ing like holes in the wall not women—their clothes—and you look again and see the brave, the noble *mujer*, the mother, the woman, the Virgin Mary of Mexico.—Tris-tessa has a huge ikon in a corner of her bedroom.

It faces the room, back to the kitchen wall, in right hand corner as you face the woesome kitchen with its drizzle showering ineffably from the roof tree twigs and hammberboards (bombed out shelter roof)—Her ikon represents the Holy Mother staring out of her blue char-aderees, her robes and Damema arrangements, at which El Indio prays devoutly when going out to get some junk. El Indio is a vendor of curios, allegedly,—I never see him on San Juan Letran selling crucifixes, I never see El Indio in the street, no Redondas, no anywhere— The Virgin Mary has a candle, a bunch of glass-fulla-wax economical burners that go for weeks on end, like Tibetan prayer-wheels the inexhaustible aid from our Amida—I smile to see this lovely ikon—

Around it are pictures of the dead—When Tristessa wants to say "dead" she clasps her hands in holy attitude, indicating her Aztecan belief in the holiness of death, by same token the holiness of the essence—So she has photo of dead Dave my old buddy of previous years now dead of high blood pressure at age 55—His vague Greek-Indian face looks out from pale indefinable photograph. I can't see him in all that snow. He's in heaven for sure, hands V-clasped in eternity ecstasy of Nirvana. That's why Tristessa keeps clasping her hands and praying, saying, too, "I love Dave," she had loved her former master—He had been an old man in love with a young girl. At 16 she was an addict. He took her off the street and, himself an addict of the street, redoubled his energies, finally made contact with wealthy junkies and showed her how to live—once a year together they'd taken hikes to Chalmas to the mountain to climb part of it on their knees to come to the shrine of piled crutches left there by pilgrims healed of disease, the thousand *tapete*-straws laid out in the mist where they sleep the night out in blankets and raincoats—returning, devout, hungry, healthy, to light new candles to the Mother and hitting the street again for their morphine—God knows where they got it.

I sit admiring that majestical mother of lovers.

THERE'S NO DESCRIBING the awfulness of that gloom in the holes in the ceiling, the brown halo of the

night city lost in a green vegetable height above the
Wheels of the Blakean adobe rooftops—Rain is blearing
now on the green endlessness of the Valley Plain north
of Actopan—pretty girls are dashing over gutters full
of pools—Dogs bark at hirshing cars—The drizzle emp-
ties eerily into the kitchen's stone Dank, and the door
glistens (iron) all shiney and wet—The dog is howling
in pain on the bed.—The dog is the little Chihuahua
mother 12 inches long, with fine little feet with black
toes and toenails, such a "fine" and delicate dog you
couldnt touch her without she'd squeal in pain—
"Y- e e e - p" All you could do was snap your finger gently
at her and allow her to nip-nose her cold little wet snout
(black as a bull's) against your fingernails and thumb.
Sweet little dog—Tristessa says she's in heat and that's
why she cries—The rooster screams beneath the bed.

All this time the rooster's been listening under the
springs, meditating, turning to look all around in his
quiet darkness, the noise of the golden humans above
" B e u - v e u - V A A?" he screams, he howls, he inter-
rupts a half a dozen simultaneous conversations raging
like torn paper above—The hen chuckles.

The hen is outside, wandering among our feet, pecking gently at the floor—She digs the people. She wants
to come up near me and rub illimitably against my pant
leg, but I dont give her encouragement, in fact havent
noticed her yet and it's like the dream of the vast mad
father of the wild barn in howling Nova Scotia with the
floodwaters of the sea about to engulf the town and
surrounding pine countrysides in the endless north—It

was Tristessa, Cruz on the bed, El Indio, the cock, the dove on the mantelpiece top (never a sound except occasional wing flap practice), the cat, the hen, and the bloody howling woman dog blacky Espana Chihuahua pooch bitch.

El Indio's eyedropper is completely full, he jabs in the needle hard and it's dull and it wont penetrate the skin and he jabs in harder and works it in but instead of wincing waits open mouthed with ecstasy and gets the dropful in, down, standing,—"You've got to do me a favor Mr. Gazookus," says Old Bull Gaines interrupting my thought, "come down to Tristessa's with me—I've run short—" but I'm bursting to explode out of sight of Mexico City with walking in the rain splashing through puddles not cursing nor interested but just trying to get home to bed, dead.

It's the raving bloody book of dreams of the cursing world, full of suits, dishonesties and written agreements. And briberies, to children for their sweets, to children for their sweets. "Morphine is for pain," I keep thinking, "and the rest is rest. It is what it is, I am what I am, Adoration to Tathagata, Sugata, Buddha, perfect in Wisdom and Compassion who has accomplished, and is accomplishing, and will accomplish, all these words of mystery."

—Reason I bring the whiskey, to drink, to crash through the black curtain—At same time a comedian in the city in the night—Bepestered by glooms and lull intervenes, bored, drinking, curtsying, crashing, "Where

I'm gonna do,"—I pull the chair up to the corner of the foot of the bed so I can sit between the kitty and the Virgin Mary. The kitty, *la gata* in Spanish, the little Tathagata of the night, golden pink colored, 3 weeks old, crazy pink nose, crazy face, eyes of green, mustachio'd golden lion forceps and whiskers—I run my finger over her little skull and she pops up purring and the little purring-machine is started for awhile and she looks around the room glad watching what we're all doing.— "She's having golden thoughts," I'm thinking.—Tristessa likes eggs otherwise she wouldnt allow a male rooster in this female establishment? How should I know how eggs are made. On my right the devotional candles flame before the clay wall.

IT'S INFINITELY WORSE than the sleeping dream I've had of Mexico City where I go dreary along empty white apartments, gray, alone, or where the marble steps of a hotel horrify me—It's the rainy night in Mexico City and I'm in the middle of Mexico Thieves Market district and El Indio is a wellknown thief and even Tristessa was a pickpocket but I dont do more than flick my backhand against the bulge of my folded money sailorwise stowed in the railroad watchpocket of my jeans—And in shirtpocket I have the travelers checks which are unstealable in a sense—That, Ah that side street where the gang of Mexicans stop me and rifle through my dufflebag and

take what they want and take me along for a drink—It's
gloom as unpredicted on this earth, I realize all the
uncountable manifestations the thinking-mind invents
to place wall of horror before its pure perfect realization
that there is no wall and no horror just Transcendental
Empty Kissable Milk Light of Everlasting Eternity's true
and perfectly empty nature.—I know everything's alright but I want proof and the Buddhas and the Virgin
Marys are there reminding me of the solemn pledge of
faith in this harsh and stupid earth where we rage our
so-called lives in a sea of worry, meat for Chicagos of
Graves—right this minute my very father and my very
brother lie side by side in mud in the North and I'm
supposed to be smarter than they are—being quick I am
dead. I look up at the others glooping, they see I've been
lost in thought in my corner chair but are pursuing
endless wild worries (all mental 100%) of their own—
They're yakking in Spanish, I only understand snatches
of that virile conversation—Tristessa keeps saying
"chinga" at every other sentence, a swearing Marine,—
she says it with scorn and her teeth bite and it makes
me worry 'Do you know women as well as you think you
do?'—The rooster is unperturbed and lets go a blast.

I TAKE OUT my whiskey bottle from the bag, the Canady
Dry, open both, and pour me a hiball in a cup—making
one too for Cruz who has just jumped outa bed to throw

up on the kitchen floor and now wants another drink, she's been in the cantina for women all day somewhere back near the whore district of Panama Street and sinister Rayon Street with its dead dog in the gutter and beggars on the sidewalk with no hats looking at you helplessly—Cruz is a little Indian woman with no chin and bright eyes and wears high heel pumps without stockings and battered dresses, what a wild crew of people, in America a cop would have to do a double take seeing them pass all be-wrongled and arguing and staggering on the sidewalk, like apparitions of poverty—Cruz takes a hiball and throws it up too. Nobody notices, El Indio is holding eyedropper in one hand and little piece of paper in the other arguing, tense necked, red, fullblast at a screaming Tristessa whose bright eyes dance to fight it out—The old lady Cruz groans from the riot of it and buries back in her bed, the only bed, under her blanket, her face bandaged and greasy, the little black dog curling against her, and the cat, and she is lamenting something, her drink sickness, and El Indio's constant harassing for more of Tristessa's supply of morphine—I gulp my drink.

Next door the mother's made the little daughter cry, we can hear her praying little woeful squeals enough to make a father's heart break and maybe it might be,— Trucks pass, buses, loud, growling, loaded to the springs with people riding to Tacuyaba and Rastro and Circumvalacion round-routeries of town—the streets of mess puddles that I am going to walk home in at 2 A M splashing without care through streetpools, looking along lone fences at the dismal glimmer of the wet rain shinning in the streetlight—The pit and horror of my grit, the Virya tense-neck muscles that a man needs to steel his teeth together to press through lonely roads of rain at night with no hope of a warm bed—My head fells and wearies to think of it. Tristessa says "How is Jack,—?—" She always asks: "Why are you so sad??— 'Muy dolorosa' " and as though to mean "You are very full of pain," for pain means *dolor*—"I am sad because all la vida es dolorosa," I keep replying, hoping to teach her Number One of the Four Great Truths,—Besides, what could be truer? With her heavy purple eyes she lids at me the nodding reprisal, 'h a - hum,' Indian-wise understanding the tone of what I said, and nodding over it, making me suspicious of the bridge of her nose where it looks evil and conniving and I think of her as a Houri Hari Salesman in the hellbottoms Kshitigarbha never dreamed to redeem.—When she looks like an evil Indian Joe of Huckleberry Finn, plotting my demise—El Indio, standing, watching through sad blackened-blue eye flesh, hard and sharp and clear the side of his face, darkly hearing that I say All Life is Sad, nods, agreeing, no comment to make to me or to anyone about it.

Tristessa is bending over the spoon boiling morphine in it with a match boilerfactory. She looks awkward and lean and you see the lean hocks of her rear, in the ki-mono-like crazydress, as she kneels prayer fashion over the bed boiling her bang over the chair which is cluttered with ashes, hairpins, cottons, Konk material like strange Mexican eyelash lippmakers and teasies and greases— one jiblet of a whole bone of junk, that, had it been knocked down would have added to the mess on the floor only a minor further amount of confusion.—"I raced to find that Tarzan," I'm thinking, remembering boyhood and home as they lament in the Mexican Saturday Night Bedroom, "but the bushes and the rocks weren't real and the beauty of things must be that they end."

I WAIL ON my cup of hiball so much they see I'm going to get drunk so they all permit me and beseech me to take a shot of morphine which I accept without fear because I am drunk—Worse sensation in the world, to take morphine when you're drunk, the result knots in your forehead like a rock and makes great pain there warring in that one field for dominion and none to be had because they've cancelled out each other the alcohol and the alkaloid. But I accept, and as soon as I begin to feel its warning effect and warm effect I look down and perceive that the chicken, the hen, wants to make friends with me—She's walking up close with bobbing neck, looking at my knee cap, looking at my hanging hands, wants to come close but has no authority—So I stick my hand out to its beak to be pecked, to let her know I'm not afraid because I trust her not to hurt me

really—which she doesn't—just stares at my hand rea-
sonably and doubtfully and suddenly almost tenderly
and I pull away my hand with a sense of the victory. She
contentedly chuckles, plucks up a piece of something
from the floor, throws it away, a piece of linen thread
hangs in her beak, she tosses it away, looks around, walks
around the golden kitchen of Time in huge Nirvana
glare of Saturday night and all the rivers roaring in the
rain, the crash inside my soul when I think of babyhood
and you watch the big adults in the room, the wave and
gnash of their shadowy hands, as they harangue about
time and responsibility, in a Golden Movie inside my
own mind without substance not even gelatinous—the
hope and horror of the void—great phantoms screech-
ing inside mind with the yawk photograph VLORK of
the Rooster as he now ups and emits from his throat
intended for open fences of Missouri explodes gunpow-
der blurts of morningshame, reverend for man—At
dawn in impenetrable bleak Oceanities of Undersunk
gloom, he blows his rosy morn Collario and still the
farmer knows it wont tend that rosy way. Then he chuckles, rooster chuckles, comments on something crazy we
might have said, and chuckles—poor sentient noticing
being, the beast he knows his time is up in the Chick-
enshacks of Lenox Avenue—chuckles like we do—yells
louder if a man, with special rooster jowls and jinglets—
Hen, his wife, she wears her adjustible hat falling from
one side of her pretty beak to the other. "Good *morn* ing
Mrs. Gazookas," I tell her, having fun by myself watching

the chickens as I'd done as a boy in New Hampshire in farmhouses at night waiting for the talk to be done and the wood to be taken in. Worked hard for my father in the Pure Land, was strong and true, went to the city to see Tathagata, leveled the ground for his feet, saw bumps everywhere and leveled the ground, he passed by and saw me and said "First level your own mind, and then the earth will be level, even unto Mount Sumeru" (the ancient name for Everest in Old Magadha) (India).

I WANTA MAKE friends with the rooster too, by now I'm sitting in front of the bed in the other chair as El Indio has just gone out with a bunch of suspicious men with mustaches one of whom stared at me curiously and with pleased proud grin as I stood with cup in hand acting drunk before the ladies for his and his friends' edification—Alone in the house with the two women I sit politely before them and we talk earnestly and eagerly about God. "My friends ees seek, I geev them shot," beautiful Tristessa of Dolours is telling me with her long damp expressive fingers dancing little India-Tinkle dances before my haunted eyes."—Eees when, *cuando*, my friend does not pays me back, don I dont care. Because" pointing up with a straight expression into my eyes, finger aloft, "my Lord pay me—and he pay me *more* —M-o-r-e"—she leans quickly emphasizing more, and I wish I could tell her in Spanish the illimitable and

inestimable blessing she will get anyway in Nirvana. But
I love her, I fall in love with her. She strokes my arm
with thin finger. I love it. I'm trying to remember my
place and my position in eternity. I have sworn off lust
with women,—sworn off lust for lust's sake,—sworn off
sexuality and the inhibiting impulse—I want to enter the
Holy Stream and be safe on my way to the other shore,
but would as lief leave a kiss to Tristessa for her hark
of my heart's sake. She knows I admire and love her
with all my heart and that I'm holding myself back. "You
have you life," she says to Old Bull (of whom in a minute)
"and I haff *mind*, mine, and Jack has hees life" indicating
me, she is giving me my life back and not claiming it for
herself as so many of the women you love do claim.—
I love her but I want to leave. She says: "I know it, a
man and women iss dead,—" "when they want to be
dead"—She nods, confirms within herself some dark
Aztecan instinctual belief, wise—a wise woman, who
would have graced the herds of Bhikshunis in very Ya-
sodhara's time and made a divine additional nun. With
her lidded eyes and clasped hands, a Madonna. It makes
me cry to realize Tristessa has never had a child and
probably never will because of her morphine sickness
(a sickness that goes on as long as the need and feeds
off the need and fills in the need simultaneously, so that
she moans from pain all day and the pain is real, like
abcesses in the shoulder and neuralgia down the side of
the head and in 1952 just before Christmas she was
supposed to be dying), holy Tristessa will not be cause

of further rebirth and will go straight to her God and
He will recompense her multibillionfold in aeons and
aeons of dead Karma time. She understands Karma, she
says: "What I do, I *reap*" she says in Spanish—"Men and
women have *errores*—errors, faults, sins, *faltas*," hu-
manbeings sow their own ground of trouble and stumble
over the rocks of their own false erroring imagination,
and life is hard. She knows, I know, you know.—"Bot—
I weeling to haff jonk—morfina—and be no-seek any
more." And she hunches her elbows with peasant face,
understanding herself in a way that I cannot and as I
gaze at her the candlelight flickers on the high cheekbones of her face and she looks as beautiful as Ava
Gardner and even better like a Black Ava Gardner, A
Brown Ava with long face and long bones and long
lowered lids—Only Tristessa hasnt got that expression
of sex-smile, it has the expression of mawkfaced down-
mouthed Indian disregard for what you think about its
own pluperfect beauty. Not that it's perfect beauty like
Ava, it's got faults, errors, but all men and women have
them and so all women forgive men and men forgive
women and go their own holy ways to death. Tristessa
loves death, she goes to the ikon and adjusts flowers and
prays,—She bends over a sandwich and prays, looking
sideways at the ikon, sitting Burmese fashion in the bed
(knee in front of knee) (down) (sitting), she makes a long
prayer to Mary to ask blessing or thanks for the food,
I wait in respectful silence, take a quick peek at El Indio,
who is also devout and even on the point of crying from

junk his eyes moist and reverent and sometimes like
especially when Tristessa removes her stockings to get
in the bed-blankets an undercurrent of reverent love
sayings under his breath ("Tristessa, O Yé, comme t'est
Belle") (which is certainly what I'm thinking but afraid
to look and watch Tristessa remove her nylons for fear
I will get a flash sight of her creamy coffee thighs and
go mad)—But El Indio is too loaded with the poison
solution of morphine to really care and follow up his
reverence for Tristessa, he is busy, sometimes busy being
sick, has a wife, two children (down the other side of
town), has to work, has to cajole stuff off Tristessa when
he himself is out (as now)—(reason for his presence in
the house)—I see the whole thing popping and paren-
thesizing in every direction, the story of that house and
that kitchen.

In the kitchen is hanging pictures of Mexican Por-
nography Girls, with black lace and big thighs and re-
vealing clouds of bosom and pelvic drapery, that I study
intently, in the right places, but the pictures (2) are all
roiled and rain-stained and roll-spanned and hanging
protruding from the wall so you have to straighten them
down to study, and even then the rain is misting down
through the cabbage leaves above and the soggy card-
board—Who might have tried to make a roof for Fel-
laheena?—"My Lord, he pay me back *more*"—

SO NOW EL INDIO is back and standing at the head
of the bed as I sit there, and I turn to look at the rooster
("to tame him")—I put my hand out exactly as I had
done for the hen and allow it to see I'm not scared if it
pecks me, and I will pat it and make it free from fear
of me—The Rooster gazes at my hand without comment,
and looks away, and looks back, and gazes at my hand
(the seminal gysmal champion who dreams a daily egg
for Tristessa that she sucks out the end after a little
puncture, fresh)—he looks at my hand tenderly but
majestically moreover as the hen can't make that same
majestical appraisal, he's crowned and cocky and can
howl, he is the King Fencer biting the duel with that
mosey morn. He chuckles at sight of my hand, meaning
Yeh and turns away—and I look proudly around to see
if Tristessa and El Indio heard my wild *estupiante*—They
rave to notice me with avid lips, "Yes we been talkin
about the ten gram-mos we gonna get tomorrar—Yeh—
" and I feel proud to've made the Rooster, now all the
little animals in the room know me and love me and I
love them though may not know them. All except The
Crooner on the roof, on the clothes closet, in the corner
away from the edge, against the wall just under the
ceiling, cozy cooing Dove is sitting in nest, ever contem-
plating the entire scene forever without comment. I look
up, my Lord is flapping his wings and coo doving white

and I look at Tristessa to know why she got a dove and
Tristessa lifts up her tender hands helplessly and looks
at me affectionately and sadly, to indicate, "It is my
Pigeon"—"my pretty white Pigeon—what can I do about
it?" "I love it so"—"It is so sweet and white"—"It never
make a noise"—"It got soch prurty eyes you look you
see the prurty eyes" and I look into the eyes of the dove
and they are dove's eyes, lidded, perfect, dark, pools,
mysterious, almost Oriental, unbearable to withstand the
surge of such purity out of eyes—Yet so much like Tristessa's eyes that I wish I could comment and tell Tristessa
'Thou hast the dove's eyes'—

Or every now and then the Dove rises and flaps her
wings for exercise, instead of flying through the bleak
air she waits in her golden corner of the world waiting
for perfect purity of death, the Dove in the grave is a
dark thing to rave—the raven in the grave is no white
light illuminating the Worlds pointing up and pointing
down throughout uppity ten sides of Eternity—Poor
Dove, poor eyes,—her breast white snow, her milk, her
rain of pity over me, her even gentle eye-gaze into mine
from rosy heights on a position in a rack and Arcabus
in the Ope Heavens of the Mind World,—rosy golden
angel of my days, and I can't touch her, wouldn't dare
get up on a chair and trap her in her corner and make
her leery human teeth-grins trying to impress it to my
bloodstained heart—her blood.

EL INDIO HAS brought sandwiches back and the little cat is going crazy for some meat and El Indio gets mad and slaps it off the bed and I throw both hands up at him "Non" "Don't do that" and he doesn't even hear me as Tristessa yells at him—the great Man Beast raging in the kitchen meat and slapping his daughter in her chair clear across the room to tumble on the floor her tears start starting as she realizes what he's done—I don't like El Indio for hitting the cat. But he isn't vicious about it, just merely reprimandatory, stern, justified, dealing with the cat, kicking the cat out of his way in the parlor as he walks to his cigars and Television—Old Father Time is El Indio, with the kids, the wife, the evenings at the supper table slapping the kids away and yornching on great meaty dinners in the dim light—"Blurp, blap," he lets go before the kids who look at him with shining and admiring eyes. Now it's Saturday night and he's dealing with Tristessa and wrangling to explain her, suddenly the old Cruz (who is not old, just 40) jumps up crying "Yeh, with our money, Si, con nuestra dinero" and repeating twice and sobbing and El Indio warns her I might understand (as I look up with imperial magnificence of unconcern tinged by regard for the scene) and as if to say "This woman is crying because you take all their money,—what is this? Russia? Mussia? Matamorapussia? as if I didn't care anyway which I couldnt. All

I wanted to do was get away. I had completely forgotten about the dove and only remembered it days later.

THE WILD WAY Tristessa stands legs spread in the middle of the room to explain something, like a junkey on a corner in Harlem or anyplace, Cairo, Bang Bombayo and the whole Fellah Ollah Lot from Tip of Bermudy to wings of albatross ledge befeathering the Arctic Coastline, only the poison they serve out of Eskimo Gloogloo seals and eagles of Greenland, ain't as bad as that German Civilization morphine she (an Indian) is forced to subdue and die to, in her native earth.

MEANWHILE THE CAT is comfortably ensconced at Cruz's face place where she lies at the foot of the bed, curled, the way she sleeps all night while Tristessa curls at the head and they hook feet like sisters or like mother and daughter and make one little bed do comfortably for two—The little pink kitkat is so certain (despite all his fleas crossing the bridge of his nose or wandering over his eyelids)—that everything is alright—that all is well in the world (at least now)—he wants to be near Cruz's face, where all is well—He (it's a little She) he doesnt notice the bandages and the sorrow and the drunksick horrors she's having, he just knows she's the lady all day her legs are in the kitchen and every now and then she dumps him food, and besides she plays with him on the bed and pretends she's gonna beat him up and holds and scolds him and he yurks in little face into little head and blinks his eyes and flaps back his ears to wait for the beating but she's only playing with him— So now he sits in front of Cruz and even though we may gesture like maniacs as we talk and occasionally a rough hand is waved right by its whiskers almost hitting it or El Indio might roughly decide to throw a newspaper on the bed and land it right on his head, still he sits digging all of us with eyes closed and curled up under Cat Buddha style, meditating among our mad endeavors like the Dove above—I wonder: "Does kittykat know there's a pigeon on the clothes closet." I wish my relatives from Lowell were here to see how people and animals live in Mexico—

But the poor little cat is one mass of fleas, but he doesnt mind, he doesnt keep scratching like American cats but just endures—I pick him up and he's just a skinny little skeleton with great balloons of fur—Everything is so poor in Mexico, people are poor, and yet everything they do is happy and carefree, no matter what is—Tristessa is a junkey and she goes about it skinny and carefree, where an American would be gloomy— But she coughs and complains all day, and by same law, at intervals, the cat explodes into furious scratching that doesnt help—

MEANWHILE I KEEP smoking, my cigarette goes out, and I reach into the ikon for a light from the candle flame, in a glass—I hear Tristessa say something that I interpret to mean "Ack, that stupid fool is using our altar for a light"—To me it's nothing unusual or strange, I just want a light—but perceiving the remark or maintaining belief in the remark without knowing what it was, I ulp and hold back and instead get a light from El Indio, who then shows me later, by quick devout prayer-ito with a piece of newspaper, getting his light indirectly and with a touch and a prayer—Perceiving the ritual I do it too, to get my light a few minutes later— I make a little French prayer: *"Excuse mué ma 'Dame"*— making emphasis on *Dame* because of Damema the Mother of Buddhas.

So I feel less guilty about my smoke and I know all of a sudden all of us will go to heaven straight up from where we are, like golden phantoms of Angels in Gold Strap we go hitch hiking the Deus Ex Machina to heights Apocalyptic, Eucalyptic, Aristophaneac and Divine—I suppose, and I wonder what the cat might think—To Cruz I say "Your cat is having golden thoughts (su gata tienes pensas de or)" but she doesnt understand for a thousand and one billion manifold reasons swimming in the swarm of her milk thoughts Buddha-buried in the stress of her illness enduring—*"What's pensas?"* she yells to the others, she doesnt know that the cat is having golden thoughts—But the cat loves her so, and stays there, little behind to her chin, purring, glad, eyes X-closed and stoopy, kitty kitkat like the Pinky I'd just lost in New York run over on Atlantic Avenue by the swerve dim madtraffics of Brooklyn and Queens, the automatons sitting at wheels automatically killing cats every day about five or six a day on the same road. "But this cat will die the normal Mexican death—by old age or disease—and be a wise old big burn in the alleys around, and you'll see him (dirty as rags) flitting by the garbage heap like a rat, if Cruz ever gets to throw it out—But Cruz won't, and so cat stays at her chin-point like a little sign of her good intentions."

EL INDIO GOES out and gets meat sandwiches and now the cat goes mad yelling and mewing for some and El Indio throws her off the bed—but Cat finally gets a bite of meat and ronches at it like a mad little Tiger and I think "If she was as big as the one in the Zoo, she'd look at me with big green eyes before eating me." I'm having the fairy tale of Saturday night, having a good time actually because of the booze and the good cheer and the careless people—enjoying the little animals—noticing the little Chihuahua pup now meekly waiting for a bite of meat or bread with her tail curled in and woe, if she ever inherits the earth it'll be because of

meek—Ears curled back and even whimpering the little
Chihuahua smalldog fear-cry—Nevertheless she's been
alternately watching us and sleeping all night, and her
own reflections on the subject of Nirvana and death and
mortals biding time till death, are of a whimpering high
frequency terrified tender variety—and the kind that
says 'Leave me alone, I am so delicate' and you leave her
alone in her little fragile shell like the shell of canoes
over the ocean deeps—I wish I could communicate to
all these creatures and people, in the flush of my moonshine goodtimes, the cloudy mystery of the magic milk
to be seen in Mind's Deep Imagery where we learn that
everything is nothing—in which case they wouldnt worry
any more, except after the instant they think to worry
again—All of us trembling in our mortality boots, born
to die, BORN TO DIE I could write it on the wall and
on Walls all over America—Dove in wings of peace, with
her Noah Menagery Moonshine eyes; dog with clitty
claws black and shiny, to die is born, trembles in her
purple eyes, her little weak bloodvessels down the ribs;
yea the ribs of Chihuahua, and Tristessa's ribs too, beautiful ribs, her with her aunts in Chihuahua also born to
die, beautiful to be ugly, quick to be dead, glad to be
sad, mad to be had—and the El Indio death, born to
die, the man, so he plies the needle of Saturday Night
every night is Saturday night and goes wild to wait, what
else can he do,—The death of Cruz, the drizzles of re-
ligion falling on her burial fields, the grim mouth planted
the satin of the earth coffin, . . . I moan to recover

all that magic, remembering my own *impending* death,
'If only I had the magic self of babyhood when I remembered what it was like before I was born, I wouldnt
worry about death now knowing both to be the same
empty dream'—But what will the Rooster say when it
dies, and someone hacks a knife at its fragile chin—And
sweet Hen, she who eats out of Tristessa's paw a globule
of beer, her beak miffling like human lips to chirn up
the milk of the beer—when she dies, sweet hen, Tristessa
who loves her will save her lucky bone and wrap it in
red thread and keep it in her belongings, nevertheless
sweet Mother Hen of our Arc of Noah Night, she the
golden purveyor and reaches so far back you can't find
the egg that prompted her outward through the first
original shell, they'll hack and whack at her tail with
hacksaws and make mincemeat out of her that you run
through an iron grinder turning handle, and would you
wonder why she trembles from fear of punishment too?
And the death of the cat, little dead rat in the gutter
with twisted yickface—I wish I could communicate to all
their combined fears of death the Teaching that I have
heard from Ages of Old, that recompenses all that pain
with soft reward of perfect silent love abiding up and
down and in and out everywhere past, present, and future in the Void unknown where nothing happens and
all simply is what it is. But they know that themselves,
beast and jackal and love woman, and my Teaching of
Old is indeed so old they've heard it long ago before my
time.

I become depressed and I gotta go home. Everyone of us, *born to die*.

BRIGHT EXPLANATION OF the crystal clarity of all the Worlds, I need, to show that we'll all be all right—The measurement of robot machines at this time is rather irrelevant or at any time—The fact that Cruz cooked with a smoky kerosene stove big pottery-fulls of carne meat-general from a whole heifer, bites of veal, pieces of veal tripe and heifer brains and heifer forehead bones . . . this wouldn't ever send Cruz to hell because no one's told her to stop the slaying, and even if someone had, Christ or Buddha or Holy Mohammed, she would still be safe from harm—though by God the heifer ain't—

The little kitty is mewing rapidly for meat—himself a little piece of quivering meat—soul eats soul in the general emptiness.

"STOP COMPLAININ!" I yell to the cat as he raves on the floor and finally jumps and joins us on the bed—The hen is rubbing her long feathery side gently imperceptibly against my shoe-tip and I can barely feel it and look in time to recognize, what a gentle touch it is from Mother Maya—She's the Magic henlayer without origin, the limitless chicken with its head cut off—The cat is mewing so violently I begin to worry for the chicken, but no the cat is merely meditating now quietly over a piece of smell on the floor, and I give the poor little fellow a whirr a purr on the thin sticky shoulders with my fingertip—Time to go, I've petted the cat, said goodbye to God the Dove, and wanta leave the heinous kitchen in the middle of a vicious golden dream—It's all taking place in one vast mind, us in the kitchen, I don't believe a word of it or a substantial atom-empty hunk of flesh of it, I see right through it, right through our fleshy forms (hens and all) at the bright amethyst future whiteness of reality—I am worried but I aint glad—"Foo," I say, and rooster looks at me, "what z he mean by *foo!*" and Rooster goes "Cork a Loodle Doo" a real Sunday morning (which it is now, 2 A M) Squawk and I see the brown corners of the dream house and remember my mother's dark kitchen long ago on cold streets in the other part of the same dream as this cold present kitchen with its drip-pots and horrors of Indian Mexico City—Cruz is feebly trying to say goodnight to me as I prepare to go, I've petted her several times a pat on the shoulder thinking that's what she wanted at the right moments and reassured her I loved her and was on her side "but I had no side of my own," I lie to myself—I've wondered what Tristessa thought of my patting her—for awhile I almost thought she was her mother, one wild moment I divined this: "Tristessa and El Indio are brother and sister, and this is their Mother, and they're driving her crazy yakking in the night about poison and morphine'—Then I realize: "Cruz is a junkey too, uses three gramos a month, she'll be on the same time and antenna of their dream trouble, moaning and groaning they'll all three go through the rest of their lives sick. Addiction and affliction. Like diseases of the mad, insane inside encephilitises of the brain where you knock out your health purposely to hold a feeling of feeble chemical gladness that has no basis in anything but the thinking-mind—Gnosis, they will certainly change me the day they try to lay morphine on me. And on ye."

Though the shot has done me some good and I haven't touched the bottle since, a kind of weary gladness has come over me tinged with wild strength—the morphine has gentlized my concerns but I'd rather not have it for the weakness it brings to my ribs,—I shall have them bashed in—"I don't want no more morphine after this," I vow, and I yearn to get away from all the morphine talk which, after sporadic listens, has finally wearied me.

I get up to go, El Indio will go with me, walk me to the corner, though at first he argues with them as though he wanted to stay or wanted something further—We go out quickly, Tristessa closes the door in back of us, I don't even give her a close look, just a glance as she closes indicating I'll see her later—El Indio and I walk vigorously down the slimey rainy aisles, turn right, and cut out to the market street, I've already commented on his black hat, and now here I am on the street with the famous Black Bastard—I've already laughed and said "You're just like Dave" (Tristessa's ex husband) "you even wear the black hat" as I'd seen Dave one time, on Redondas—in the moil and wild of a warm Friday night with buses parading slowly by and mobs on the sidewalk; Dave hands the package to his boy, the seller calls the cop, cop comes running, boy hands it back to Dave, Dave says 'Okay take it and ron' and tosses it back and boy hits ledge of a flying bus and hangs in to the crowd with his loins his body hanging over the street and his arms rigidly holding the bus door pole, the cops can't catch, Dave meanwhile has vamoosed into a saloon, removed his legendary black hat, and sat at the counter with other men looking straight ahead—cops no find—I had admired Dave for his guts, now admire El Indio for *his*— As we come out of the Tristessa tenement he lets loose a whistle and a shout at a bunch of men on the corner, we walk right along and they spread and we come up to the corner and walk right on talking, I've not paid attention to what he's done, all I wanta do is go straight home—It's started to drizzle—

"YA VOY DORMIENDO, I go sleep now" says El Indio putting his palms together at side of his mouth—I say "Okay" then he makes a further elaborate statement I think repeating in words what done before by sign, I fail to acknowledge complete understanding of his new statement, he disappointedly says "Yo un untiende" (you dont understand) but I do understand that he wants to

go home and go to bed—"Okay" I say—We shake—We
then go through an elaborate smiling routine on the
streets of man, in fact on broken cobbles of Redondas—

To reassure him I give him a parting smile and start
off but he keeps alertly watching every flicker of my
smiler and eyelash, I can't turn away with an arbitrary
leer, I want to smile him on his way, he replies by smiles
of his own equally elaborate and psychologically cor-
roborative, we swing informations back and forth with
crazy smiles of farewell, so much so, El Indio stumbles
in the extreme strain of this, over a rock, and throws
still a further parting smile of reassurance capping my
own, till no end in sight, but we stumble in our opposite
directions as though reluctant—which reluctance lasts
a brief second, the fresh air of the night hits your new-
born solitude and both you and your Indio go off in a
new man and the smile, part of the old, is removed, no
longer necessita—He to his home, I to mine, why smile
about it all night long except in company—The drear-
iness of the world politely—

I GO DOWN the Wild Street of Redondas, in the rain,
it hasn't started increasing yet, I push through and dodge
through moils of activity with whores by the hundreds
lined up along the walls of Panama Street in front of
their crib cells where big Mamacita sits near the cocina
pig pottery, as you leave they ask a little for the pig who

also represents the kitchen, the chow, *cocina*,—Taxis are
slanting by, plotters are aiming for their dark, the whores
are nooking the night with their crooking fingers of
Come On, young men pass and give em the once over,
arm in arm in crowds the young Mexicans are Casbah
buddying down their main girl street, hair hanging over
their eyes, drunk, borracho, longlegged brunettes in
tight yellow dresses grab them and sock their pelvics in,
and pull their lapels, and plead—the boys wobble—the
cops down the street pass idly like figures on little wheel-
thucks rolling by invisibly under the sidewalk—One look
through the bar where the children gape and one
through the whoreboy bar of queers where spidery heroes perform whore dances in turtleneck sweaters for
assembled critical elders of 22—look through both holes
and see the eye of the criminal, criminal in heaven.—I
plow through digging the scene, swinging my bag with
the bottle in it, I twist and give the whores a few twisting
looks as I walks, they send me stereotyped soundwaves
of scorn from cussin doorways—I am starving, I start
eating El Indio's sandwich he gave me which at first I'd
sought to refuse so as to leave it for the cat but El Indio
insisted it was a present for me, so I nakedly breast-high
in one delicate hold as I walk along the street—seeing
the sandwich I begin to eat it—finishing it, I start buying
tacos as I run by, any kind, any stand where they yell
"Joven!"—I buy stinking livers of sausages chopped in
black white onions steaming hot in grease that crackles
on the inverted fender of the grille—I munch down on

heats and hotsauce salsas and come to devouring whole
mouthloads of fire and rush along—nevertheless I buy
another one, further, two, of broken cow-meat hacked
on the woodblock, head and all it seems, bits of grit and
gristle, all mungied together on a mangy tortilla and
chewed down with salt, onions, and green leaf—diced—
a delicious sandwich when you get a good stand—The
stands are 1,2,3 in a row a half mile down the street,
tragically lit by candles and dim bulbs and strange lan-
terns, the whole of Mexico a Bohemian Adventure in
the great outdoor plateau night of stones, candle and
mist—I pass Plaza Garibaldi the hot spot of the police,
strange crowds are grouping in narrow streets around
quiet musicians that only later faintly you hear corneting
round the block—Marimbas are drumming in the big
bars—Rich men, poor men, in wide hats mingle—Come
out of swinging doors spitting cigar putts and clapping
big hands over their jock as though they were about to
dive in a cold brook—guilty—Up the side streets dead
buses waddling in the mud holes, spots of fiery yellow
whoredress in the dark, assembled leaners and up
against the wall lovers of the loving Mexican night—
Pretty girls passing, every age, all the comic Gordos and
me turn big heads to watch them, they're too beautiful
to bear—

I rock right by the Post Office, cross the bottom of
Juarez, the Palace of Fine Arts sinking nearby,—yoke
myself to San Juan Letran and fall to hiking up fifteen
blocks of it fast passing delicious places where they make
the churros and cut you hot salt sugar butter bites of

fresh hot donut from the grease basket, that you crunch
freshly as you cover the Peruvian night ahead of your
enemies on the sidewalk—All kinds of crazy gangs are
assembled, chief gleeful leaders getting high on gang
leadership wear crazy woollen Scandanavian Ski hats
over their zoot paraphenalias and Pachuco haircuts—
Other day here I'd passed a gang of children in a gutter
their leader dressed as a clown (with nylon stocking over
head) and wide rings painted around the eyes, the littler
kids have imitated him and attempted similar clown out-
fits, the whole thing gray and blackened eyes with white
loops, like silks of great racetracks the little gang of
Pinocchioan heroes (and Genet) paraphernaliaing on the
street curb, an older boy making fun of the Clown Hero
"What are you doing clowning, Clown Hero?—There
ain't no Heaven anywhere?" "There ain't no Santa Claus
of Clown Heroes, mad boy"—Other gangs of semi-hips-
ters hide in front of nightclub bars with wronks and
noise inside, I fly by with one quick Walt Whitman look
at all that file deroll—It starts raining harder, I've got
a long way to go walking and pushing that sore leg right
along in the gathering rain, no chance no intention whatever of hailing a cab, the whiskey and the Morphine
have made me unruffled by the sickness of the poison
in my heart.

WHEN YOU HAVE no more numbers in Nirvana then
there won't be such a thing as "numberless" but the

crowds on San Juan Letran were like numberless—I say
"Count all these sufferings from here to the end of the
endless sky which is no sky and see how many you can
add together to make a figure to impress the Boss of
Dead Souls in the Meat Manufactory in city City CITY
everyone of them in pain and born to die, milling in the
streets at 2 A M underneath those imponderable skies"—
their enormous endlessness, the sweep of the Mexican
plateau away from the Moon—living but to die, the sad
song of it I hear sometimes on my roof in the Tejado
district, rooftop cell, with candles, waiting for my Nirvana or my Tristessa—neither come, at noon I hear "La
Paloma" being played on mental radios in the fallways
between the tenement windows—the crazy kid next door
sings, the dream is taking place right now, the music is
so sad, the French horns ache, the high whiney violins
and the deberratarra-rabaratarara of the Indian Spanish
announcer. Living but to die, here we wait on this shelf,
and up in heaven is all that gold open caramel, ope my
door—Diamond Sutra is the sky.

I crash along drunkenly and bleakly and hard with
kicking feet over the precarious sidewalk slick of vegetable oil Tehuantepec, green sidewalks, swarmed with
scumworm invisible but in high—dead women hiding
in my hair, passing underneath the sandwich and chair—
"You're nuts!" I yell to the crowds in English "You don't
know what in a hell you're doing in this eternity bell
rope tower swing to the puppeteer of Magadha, Mara
the Tempter, insane, . . . And you all eagle and you bea-

gle and you buy—All you bingle you baffle and you lie—
You poor motherin bloaks pourin through the juice
parade of your Main Street Night you don't know that
the Lord has arranged everything in sight." "Including
your death." "And nothing's happening. I am not me,
you are not ye, they unnumbered are not they, and One
Un-Number Self there is no such thing."

I pray at the feet of man, waiting, as they.

As they? As Man? As he? There is no He. There is
only' the unsayable divine word. Which is not a Word,
but a Mystery.

At the root of the Mystery the separation of one world
from another by a sword of light.—

The winners of tonight's ball game in the open mist
outside Tacabatabavac are romping by in the street
swinging their baseball bats at the crowd showing how
great they can hit and the crowd walks unconcernedly
around because they are children not juvenile delin-
quents. They pull their beak baseball hats tight-hawk
down their faces, in the drizzle, tapping their glove they
wonder "Did I make a bad play in the fifth inning? Didn't
I make it up with that *heet* in the seventh inning?"

AT THE END of San Juan Letran is that last series of
bars that end in a ruined mist, fields of broken adobe,
no bums hidden, all wood, Gorky, Dank, with sewers
and puddles, ditches in the street five feet deep with

water in the bottom—powdery tenements against the
light of the nearby city—I watch the final sad bar-doors,
where flashes of women golden shining lace behinds I
can see and feel like flying in yet like a bird in flight
twist on. Kids are in the doorway in goof suits, the band
is wailing a chachacha inside, everybody's knee is knocking to bend as they pop and wail with the mad music,
the whole club is rocking, *down*, an American Negro
walking with me would have said "These cats are stoning
themselves on some real hip kicks, they are goofing all
the time, they wail, they spend all the time knocking and
knocking for that *bread*, for that *girl*, they're up in against
the doorways, man, wailing all—you know? They don't
know when to stop. It's like Omar Khayyam, I wonder
what the vintners buy, one half so precious, as what they
sell." (My boy Al Damlette.)

I TURN OFF at these last bars and it really starts raining
hard and I walk fast as I can and come to a big puddle
and jump out of it all wet and jump right in again and
cross it—The morphine prevents me from feeling the
wet, my skin and limbs are numb,—like a kid when he
goes skating in winter, falls through ice, runs home with
skates under his arm so he won't catch cold, I kept plow-
ing through the Pan American rain and above is the
gigantic roar of a Pan American Airplane coming in to
land at Mexico City Airport with passengers from New

York looking for to find the other end of dreams. I look up into the drizzle and watch their tail firespark—you won't find me landing over great cities and all I do is clutch the side of the seat and wobble as the air pilot expertly leads us into a tremendous flaming crash against the side of warehouses in the slum district of Old Indian Town—what? with all them rat tat tans with revolvers in their pockets pushing through my foggy bones looking for something made of gold, and then rats gnaw ya.

I'd rather walk than ride the airplane, I can fall on the ground flat on my face and die that way.—With a watermelon under my arm. *Mira.*

I COME UP gorgeous Orizaba Street (after crossing wide muddy parks near Ciné Mexico and the dismal trolley street called after dismal General Obregon in the rainy night, with roses in his mother's hair—) Orizaba Street has a magnificent fountain and pool in a green park at a round O-turn in residential splendid shape of stone and glass and old grills and scrolly worly lovely majesties that when looked at by the moon blend with magic inner Spanish gardens of an architecture (if architecture you will) designed for lovely nights at home. Andalusian in intention.

The fountain is not spraying water at 2 A M and as though it would have to, in the driving rain, and me rolling by there sitting on my railroad switchblock pass-

ing over pinking sparking switches on tracks of under-
neath-the-earth like the cops on the little whorestreet 35
blocks back and way downtown—

It's the dismal rainy night caught up with me—my
hair is dripping water, my shoes are slopping—but I
have my jacket on, and it is soaking on the outside—but
it is rain repellent—"Why I bought it back in the Rich-
mond Bank" I'm tellin heroes about it later, in a littlekid
dream.—I run on home, walking past the bakery where
they don't at 2 A M anymore make latenight donuts,
twisters taken out of ovens and soaked in syrup and sold
to you through the bakery window for two cents apiece
and I'd buy baskets of them in my younger days—closed
now, rainy night Mexico City of the present contains no
roses and no fresh hot donuts and it's bleak. I cross the
last street, slow down and relax letting out breath and
stumbling on my muscles, now I go in, death or no death,
and sleep the sweet sleep of white angels.

But my door is locked, my street door, I have no key
for it, all lights are out, I stand there dripping in the
rain with no place to dry up and sleep—I see there's a
light in Old Bull Gaines' window and I go over and
amazedly look in, just see his golden curtain, I realize
"If I can't get in my own place then I'll just knock on
Bull's window and sleep in his easy chair." Which I do,
knocking, and he comes out of the dark establishment
of about 20 people and in his bathrobe walks through
the little bit of rain between building and the door—
comes and snaps open the iron door. I go in after him—
"Can't go in my own place" I say—He wants to know

what Tristessa said about tomorrow, when they get
more stuff from the Black Market, the Red Market, the
Indian Market—So it's alright with Old Bull I sleep and
stay in his room—"Till the street door is opened at 8
A M" I add, and suddenly decide to curl up on the floor
with a flimsy coverlet, which, instantly as done, is like
a bed of soft fleece and I lay there divine, legs all tired
and clothes partly wet (am wrapped in Old Bull's big
towel robe like a ghost in a Turkish bath) and the whole
journey in the rain done, all I have to do is lie dreaming
on the floor. I curl up and start sleeping. In the middle
of the night now, with the small yellowbulb on, and rain
crashing outside, Old Bull Gaines has closed shutters
tight, is smoking cigarette after cigarette and I can't
breathe in the room and he's coughing "Ke-he!" the dry
junkey cough, like a protest, like yelling *Wake Up!*—he
lies there, thin, emaciated, long nosed, strangely handsome and gray haired and lean and mangy 22 in his
derelict worldling ("student of souls and cities" he calls
himself) decapitated and bombed out by morphine
frame—Yet all the guts in the world. He starts munching
on candy, I lay there waking up realizing that Old Bull
is munching on candy noisily in the night—All the sides
to this dream—Annoyed, I glance anxiously around and
see him myorking and monching on condy after condy,
what a preposterous thing to do at 4 A M in your bed—
Then at 4:30 he's up and boiling down a couple of cap-
sules of morphine in a spoon,—you see him, after the
shot has been sucked in and siphoned out, with big glad
tongue licking so he can spit on the blackened bottom

of the spoon and rub it clean and silver with a piece of paper, using, to really polish the spoon, a pinch of ashes—And he lays back, feeling it a little, it takes ten minutes, a muscle bang,—by about twenty minutes he might feel alright—if not, there he is rustling in his drawer waking me up again, he's looking for his goofballs—"So he can sleep."

So *I* can sleep. But no. Immediately he wants another jolt of some kind, he ups and opes his drawer and pulls out a tube of codeine pills and counts out ten and pops that in with a slug of cold coffee from his old cup that sits on the chair by the bed—and he endures in the night, with the light on, and lights further cigarettes—At some time or other, around dawn, he falls asleep—I get up after some reflections at 9 or 8, or 7, and quickly put my wet clothes on to rush upstairs to my warm bed and dry clothes—Old Bull is sleeping, he finally made it, Nirvana, he's snoring and he's out, I hate to wake him up but he'll have to lock himself in, with his bolt and slider—It's gray outside, rain has finally stopped after heaviest surge at dawn. 40,000 families were flooded out in the Northwestern part of Mexico City that storm. Old Bull, far from floods and storms with his needles and his powders beside the bed and cottons and eyedroppers and paraphernalias—"When you got morphine, you dont need anything else, me boy," he says to me in the daytime all combed and high sitting in his easy chair with papers the picture of glad health—"Madame Poppy, I call her. When you've got Opium you've got

all you need.—All that good *O* goes down in your veins
and you feel like singing Hallelujah!" And he laughs.
"Bring me Grace Kelly on this chair, Morphine on that
chair, I'll take Morphine."

"Ava Gardner *too*?"

"Ava GVavna and all the bazotzkas in all the countries
so far—if I can have my M in the morning and my M
in the afternoon and my M in the evening before going
to bed, I dont even need to know what time it is on the
City Hall Clock—" He tells me all this and more nodding
vigorously and sincerely. His jaw quivers with emotion.
"Why for krissakes if I had no junk I'd be bored to death,
I'd die of *boredom*" he complains, almost crying—"I read
Rimbaud and Verlaine, I know what I'm talking about—
Junk is the only thing I want—You've never been junksick, you don't know what it's like—Boy when you wake
up in the morning sick and take a good bang, boy, that
feels good." I can picture myself and Tristessa waking
up in our nuptial madbed of blankets and dogs and cats
and canaries and dots of whoreplant in the coverlet and
naked shoulder to shoulder (under the gentle eyes of
the Dove) she shoots me in or I shoot myself in a big
bang of waterycolored poison straight into the flesh of
your arm and into your system which it instantly pro-
claims *its*—you feel the weak fall of your body to the
disease in the solution—but never having been junksick,
I don't know the horror of the disease—A story Old Bull
could tell much better than I—

HE LETS ME out, but not until he's muttered and sput-
tered out of bed—holding his pajamas and bathrobe,
pushing in his belly where it hurts, where some kind of
hernia cave-in annoys him,—poor sick fella, almost 60
years old and hanging on to his diseases without both-
ering anybody—Born in Cincinnati, brought up in the
Red River Steamboats. (redlegged? his legs as white as
snow)—

I see that it's stopped raining and I'm thirsty and have
drunk Old Bull's two cups of water (boiled, and kept in
a jar)—I go across the street in my damp sopping shoes
and buy an ice-cold Spur Cola and gobble it down on
my way to my room—The skies are opening up, there
might be sunshine in afternoon, the day is almost wild
and Atlantican, like a day at sea off the coast of the Firth
of Scotland—I yell imperial flags in my thoughts and
rush up the two flights to my room, the final flight a
ricket of iron tin-spans creaking and cracking on nails
and full of sand, I get on the hard adobe floor of the
roof, the Tejado, and walk on slippery little puddles
around the air of the courtyard rail only two foot high
so you can just easily fall down three flights and crack
your skull on tile Espaniala floors where Americans
gnash and fight sometimes in raucous parties early in
the twilight of the morning,—I could fall, Old Bull almost fell over when he lived on the roof a month, the

children sit on the soft stone of the 2 foot rail and goof
and talk, all day running around the thing and skidding
and I never like to watch—I come to my room around
two curves of the Hole and unlock my padlock which
is hooked to decaying halfout nails (one time left the
room open and unattended all day)—I go in and jam
the door in the rain damp wood and rain has swollen
the wood and the door barely tightens at the top—I get
in my dry hobo pants and two big hobo shirts and go
to bed with thick socks on and finish the Spur and lay
it on the table and say "Ah" and wipe the back of my
mouth and look awhile at holes in my door showing the
outside Sunday morning sky and I hear churchbells
down Orizaba lane and people are going to church and
I'm going to sleep and I'll make up for it later, goodnight.

"BLESSED LORD, THOU lovedest all sentient life."

Why do I have to sin and do the sign of the Cross?

"Not one of the vast accumulation of conceptions from
beginningless time, through the present and into the
never ending future, not one of them is graspable."

It's the old question of "Yes life's not real" but you
see a beautiful woman or something you can't get away
from wanting because it is there in front of you—This
beautiful woman of 28 standing in front of me with her
fragile body ("I put thees in my neck [a dicky] so nobody
look and see my beautiful body," she thinks she jokes,

not regarding herself as beautiful) and that face so expressive of the pain and loveliness that went no doubt
into the making of this fatal world,— a beautiful sunrise,
that makes you stop on the sands and gaze out to sea
hearing Wagner's Magic Fire Music in your thoughts—
the fragile and holy countenance of poor Tristessa, the
tremulous bravery of her little junk-racked body that a
man could throw up in the air ten feet—the bundle of
death and beauty—all pure Form standing in front of
me, all the racks and tortures of sexual beauty, the breast,
the limb of the middle body, the whole huggable mess
of a woman some of them even though 6 feet high you
can slumber on their bellies in the night like a nap on
a dreaming bankside of a woman—Like Goethe at 80,
you know the futility of love and you shrug—You shrug
away the warm kiss, the tongue and lips, the tug at the
thin waist, the whole warm floating thing against you
held tight—the little woman—for which rivers flow and
men fall down stepladders—The thin cold long brown
fingers of Tristessa, slow, and casual and lazy, like the
meeting of lips—The Tristessa Spanish Night of her
deep love hole, the bullfights in her dreams of you, the
lazy rainy rose against the idle cheek—And all the con-
comitant lovelinesses of a lovely woman a young man
in a far-off country should yearn to stay for—I was trav-
eling around in circles in North America in many a gray
tragedy.

I STAND LOOKING at Tristessa, she's come to visit me in my room, she won't sit down, she stands and talks— in the candle light she is excited and eager and beautiful and radiant—I sit down on the bed, looking down on the stony floor, while she talks—I don't even listen to what she's saying, about junk, Old Bull, how she's tired— "I go to the do it to-*morra*—TO-MORRAR—" she taps to emphasize me with her hand, so I have to say "Yeh Yeh go ahead" and she goes on with her story, which I don't understand—I just can't look at her for fear of thoughts I'll get—But she takes care of all of that for me, she says "Yes, we are in pain—" I say "La Vida es dolor" (life is pain), she agrees, she says life is love too. "When you got one million pesos I dont care how many, they dont move"—she says, indicating my paraphernalia of leather-covered scriptures and Sears Roebuck enve- lopes with stamps and airmail envelopes inside—as though I had a million pesos hiding in time in my floor— "A million pesos does not move—but when you got the friend, the friend give it to you in the bed" she says, legs spread a little, pumping with her loins at the air in the direction of my bed to indicate how much better a human being is than a million paper pesos—I think of the inex- pressible tenderness of receiving this holy friendship from the sacrificial sick body of Tristessa and I almost feel crying or grabbing her and kissing her—A wave of loneliness passes over me, remembering past loves and bodies in beds and the unbeatable surge when you go into your beloved deep and the whole world goes with you—Though we know that Mara the Tempter is evil, his fields of temptation are innocent—How could Tristessa, rousing passion in me, have anything to do, except as a field of merit or a dupe of innocence or a material witness to my murderous lust, how could she be blamed and how could she be sweeter than standing there explaining my love directly with her pantomiming thighs. She's high, she keeps trying at the lapel of her kimono (underneath's a slip that shows) and trying to attach it unattachably to an inexistent button of the coat. I look into her eyes deep, meaning "Would you be my friend like that?" and she looks straight at me pools of neither this or that, her combination of reluctance to break her personal disgust covenant moreover lodged in the Virgin Mary, and her love of wish-for-me, makes her as mysterious as the Tathagata whose form is described as being as inexistent, rather as inscrutable as the direction in which a put-out fire has gone. I can't get a yes or no out of her eyes for the time I allot to them. Very nervous, I sit, stand, sit, she stands explaining further things. I am amazed by the way her skin wrinkles O so sensitively down the bridge of her nose in even clean lines, and her little laugh of delight that comes so rarely and so's littlegirlish, child of glee,—It's all my own sin if I make a play for her.

I WANT TO take her in both hands by the waist and pull her slowly close with a few choice words of sudden endearment like "Mi gloria angela" or "Mi whichever it is" but I have no language to cover my embarrassment—Worst of all, would it be, to have her push me aside and say "No, no, no" like disappointed mustachio'd heroes in French movies being turned out by the little blonde who is the brakeman's wife, by a fence, in smoke, midnight, in the French railroad yards, and I turn away big pained loverface and apologize,—going away thence with the sensation that I have a beastly streak in me I didn't notice, conceptions common to all young lovers and old. I don't want to disgust Tristessa—It would horrify me to cause her ruinous fleshpetal tender secrets and have her wake up in the morning lodged against the back of some unwelcome man who loves by night and sleeps it off, and wakes up blearing to shave and by his very presence causes consternation where before there was absolute perfect purity of nobody.

But what I've missed when I don't get that friend lunge of the lover's body, coming right at me, all mine, but it was a slaughterhouse for meat and all you do is bend to wreak havocs in somethings-gotta-give of girlihood.—When Tristessa was 12 years old suitors twisted her arm in the sun outside the mother's cooking door—I've seen it a million times, in Mexico the young men want the young girls—Their birthrate is terrific—They turn em out wailing and dying by the golden tons in vats of semiwinery messaferies of oy Ole Tokyo birthcrib.— I lost track of my thought there,—

Yes, the thighs of Tristessa and the golden flesh all mine, what am I a Caveman? Am a Caveman.

Caveman buried deep under ground.

It would just be the coronna of her cheeks pulsing to mouth, and my rememberance of her splendid eyes, like sitting in a box the lovely latest in France enters the crashing orchestra and I turn to Monsieur next to me whispering "She is *splendide*, non?"—With Johnny Walker Scotch in my tuxedo coatpocket.

I stand up. I must see her.

POOR TRISTESSA IS swaying there explaining all her troubles, how she hasn't got enough money, she's sick, she'll be sick in the morning and in the look of her eye I caught perhaps the gesture of a shadow of acceptance of the idea of me as a lover—Only time I ever saw Tristessa cry, was when she was junk sick on the edge of Old Bull's bed, like a woman in the back pew of a church in daily novena she dabs at her eyes—She points to the sky again, "If my friend dont pay me back," looking at me straight, "my Lord pay me back—*more*" and I can feel the spirit enter the room as she stands, waiting with her finger pointed up, on her spread legs, confidently, for

her Lord to pay her back—"So I geev every-things I
have to my friend, and eef he doan pay me back"—she
shrugs—"my Lord pay me back"—standing alert again—
"*More*" and as the spirit swims around the room I can
tell the effective mournful horror of it (her reward is
so thin) now I see radiating from the crown of her head
innumerable hands that have come from all ten quarters
of the Universe to bless her and pronounce her Bodhisat
for saying and knowing that so well.

Her Enlightenment is perfect,—"And we are nothing,
you and me"—she pokes at my chest, "Jew—Jew—"
(Mexican saying "You")"—and me"—pointing at herself—"We are *nothing*. Tomorrar we may be die, and so
we are nothing—" I agree with her, I feel the strangeness
of that truth, I feel we are two empty phantoms of light
or like ghosts in old haunted-house stories diaphanous
and precious and white and not-there,—She says "I know
you want to sleep."

"No no" I say, seeing she wants to leave—

"I go to it sleep, early in the mawnins I go get see for
the mans and I get the morfina and com bock for Old
Bool"—and since we are *nada*, nothing, I forget what
she said about friends all lost in the beauty of her strange
intelligent imagery, every bit true—"She's an Angel," I
think secretly, and escort her to the door with movement
of arm as she leans to the door talking to go out—We
are careful not to touch each other—I tremble, once I
jumped a mile when her fingertip hit my knee in conversations, at chairs—the first afternoon I'd seen her,

in dark glasses, in the sunny afternoon window, by a
candle light lit for kicks, sick kicks of life, smoking, beautiful, like the Owner Damsel of Las Vegas, or the Rev-
olutionary Heroine of Marlon Brando Zapata Mexico—
with Culiacan heroes and all—That's when she got me—
In afternoon space of gold the look, the sheer beauty,
like silk, the children giggling, me blushing, at guy's
house, where we first found Tristessa and started all
this—Sympaticus Tristessa with her heart a gold gate,
I'd first dug to be an evil enchantress—I'd run across
a Saint in Modern Mexico and here I was fantasizing
dreams away about foreordained orders for nothing and
necessary betrayals—the betrayal of the old father when
he entices by ruse the three little crazy kids screaming
and playing in the burning house, "I'll give each one
your favorite cart," out they come running for the carts,
he gives them the High Incomparable Great Cart of the
Single Vehicle White Bullock which they're too young
to appreciate—with that greatcart command, he'd made
me an offer—I look at Tristessa's leg and decide to avoid
the issue of fate and rest beyond heaven.

I play games with her fabulous eyes and she longs to
be in a monastery.

"LEAVE TRISTESSA ALONE" I say, anyway, like I'd
say "Leave the kitty alone, don't hurt it"—and I open
her the door, so we can go out, at midnight, from my

room—In my hand I stumble-awkwardly hold big rail-road brakeman lantern to her feet as we descend the perilous needless to say steps, she'd almost tripped coming up, she moaned and she groaned coming up, she smiled and minced with her hand on her skirt going down, with that majestical lovely slowness of woman, like a Chinese Victoria.

"We are nothing."

"Tomorrow we may be die."

"We are nothing."

"You and Me."

I politely lead all the way down by light and lead her out to street where I hail her a white taxi for her home.

Since beginningless time and into the never-ending future, men have loved women without telling them, and the Lord has loved them without telling, and the void is not the void because there's nothing to be empty of.

Art there, Lord Star?—Diminished is the drizzle that broke my calm.

PART TWO

A Year Later . . .

DIMINISH'D NEVER IS the drizzle that broke no calm—I didnt tell her I loved her but when I left Mexico I began to think on her and then I began to tell her I loved her in letters, and almost did, and she wrote too, pretty Spanish letters, saying I was sweet, and please hurry back—I hurried back too late, I should have come back in the Spring, almost did, had no money, just touched the border of Mexico and felt that vomity feeling of Mexico—went on to California and lived in a shack with young monk Buddhist type visitors every day and went north to Desolation Peak and spent a summer surling in the Wilderness, eating and sleeping alone—said, "Soon I go back, to the warm arms of Tristessa"—but waited too long.

O Lord, why have you done this to your angel-selves, this blight life, this ugh raggedy crap scene full of puke and thieves and dying?—couldnt you have placed us in

a dismal heaven where all was glad anyhow?—Art thou
Masochist, Lord, art thou Indian Giver, art thou Hater?

Finally I was back in Bull's room after a four thousand
mile voyage from the mountain peak near Canada, a
terrible enough trip in itself, not worth moot herein—
and he went out and got her.

Already he'd warned me: "I dont know what's the
matter with her, she's changed in the past two weeks,
the *past week* even—"

"Is that because she knew I was coming?" I thought
darkly—

"She throws fits and hits me over the head with coffee
cups and loses my money and falls in the street—"

"What's the *matter* with her?"

"Goofballs—I told her not to take too many—You
know it takes an old junkey with many years of expe-
rience to know how to handle sleeping pills,—she wont
listen, she dont know how to use em, three, four, sometimes five, once twelve, it's not the same Tristessa—What
I wanta do is *marry* her and get my citizenship, see, you
think that's a good idea?—After all, she's my life, I'm
her life—"

I could see Old Bull had fallen in love—with a woman
not named Morphina.

"I never touch her—it's just a marriage of conve-
nience—you know what I mean—I cant be getting stuff
on the black market myself, I dont know how, I need
her and she needs my money."

Bull got $150 a month from a trust fund established
by his father before he died—his father had loved him,

and I could know why, for Bull is a sweet and tender person, though just a little of the con man, for years in New York he supported his junk habit by stealing about $30 every day, twenty years—He'd been in jail a few times when they'd found him with wrong merchandise— In jail he was always the librarian, he is a great scholar, in many ways, with a marvelous interest in history and anthropology and of all things French Symbolist poetry, Mallarmé above all—I'm not talking of the other Bull who is the great writer who wrote "Junkey"—This is another Bull, older, almost 60, I wrote poems in his room all last summer when Tristessa was *mine, mine*, and I wouldnt take her—I had some silly ascetic or celibacious notion that I must not touch a woman—My touch might have saved her—

Now too late—

He brings her home and right away I see something is wrong—She comes tottering in on his arm and gives a weak (thank God for that) smile and holds out her arm rigidly, I dont know what to do but hold her arm up, "What's the matter with Tristessa is she sick?"

"All last month she was paralyzed down one whole leg and her arms were covered with cysts, O she was an awful sick girl last month"

"What's the matter with her now?"

"Shh—let her sit down—"

Tristessa is holding me and slowly levels her sweet brown cheek against mine, with a rare smile, and I'm playing the befuddled American almost consciously—

Look, I'll save her yet—

TROUBLE IS, WHAT would I do with her once I'd won her?—it's like winning an angel in hell and you are then entitled to go down with her to where it's worse or maybe there'll be light, some, down there, maybe it's me's crazy—

"She's going crazy," says Bull, "those goofballs'll do it to everybody, to you, anybody I dont care who."

In fact Bull himself took too many two nights later and proved it—

The problem of junkies, narcotic addicts bless their soul, bless their quiet thoughtful souls, is to get it—On all sides they're balked, they are continually unhappy—"If the government gave me enough morphine every day I would be completely happy and I would be completely willing to work as a male nurse in a hospital—I even sent the government my ideas on the subject, in a letter in 1938 from Lexington, how to solve the narcotic problem, by putting junkies to work, with their daily doses, cleaning the subways, anything—as long as they get their medicine they're all right, just like any other sick people—It's like alcoholics, they need medicine—"

I cant remember everything that happened except for last night so fateful, so horrible, so sad and mad—Better to do it that way, why build up?

IT ALL STARTED out with Bull being out of morphine, sick, a little too many goofballs he'd taken (secanols) to make up for the morphine lack and so he is acting like a baby, sloppy, like senile, not quite as bad as the night he slept in my bed on the roof because Tristessa had gone mad and was breaking everything in his room and hitting him and falling on the floor right on her head, goofballs she bought in a drugstore, Bull would give her no more—The anxious landladies are hovering at the door thinking we're beating her up but she's beating us up—

The things she said to me, what she really thought of me, now came out, a year later, a year too late, and all I should have done was *tell her* I loved her—She accused me of being a filthy teahead, she ordered me out of Bull's room, she tried to hit me with a bottle, she tried to take my tobacco pouch and keep it, I had to struggle with her—Bull and I hid the bread knife under the rug—She just sits there on the floor like an idiot baby, doodling with objects—She accuses me of trying to smoke marijuana out of my tobacco pouch but it is only Bull Durham tobacco for my roll-me-owns because commercial cigarettes have a chemical in them to keep them firm that damaged my susceptible phlebitic veins and arteries—

So Bull is afraid she'll kill him in the night, we cant get her out, previously (a week ago) he'd called cops and

ambulances and even they wouldnt get her out, Mexico—So he comes sleep in my new room bed, with clean
sheets, forgets that he's already taken two goofballs and
takes two more and thereupon goes blind, cant find his
cigarettes, gropes and knocks down everything, pees in
the bed, spills coffee I bring him, I have to sleep on the
floor of stone among bedbugs and cockroaches, I revile
him all night poutingly: "Look what you're doing to my
nice clean bed"

"I cant help it—I gotta find another cap—Is this a
cap?" He holds up a matchstick and thinks it's a capsule
of morphine. "Bring me your spoon"—He's going to
boil it down and shoot it—Lord—In the morning at gray
time he finally leaves and goes down to his room, stumbling with all his things including a Newsweek he could
have never read—I dump his cans of pee in the toilet,
it's all pure blue like the blue Sir of Joshua Reynolds,
I think: "MY GOD, he's gotta be dying!" but turns out
they were cans of washing blueing—Meanwhile Tristessa
has slept and feels better and somehow they stumble
around and get their shots and next day she returns
tapping in Bull's window, pale and beautiful, no more
an Aztec witch, and apologizes sweetly—

"She'll be back on goofballs in a week," says Bull—
"But I'm not giving her any more"—He swallows one
himself—

"Why do *you* take em!" I yell.

"Because I know how, I've been a junkey for forty
years"

Comes then the fateful night—

I've already finally in a cab and once on the street told Tristessa I love her—"Yo te amo"—No reply—She lies to Bull and tells him I propositioned her saying "You've slept with a lot of men, why not sleep with me"—No such thing I ever said, just "Yo te amo"—Because I do love her—But what to do with her—She never used to lie before the goofballs—In fact she used to pray and go to church—

I've given up on Tristessa and this afternoon, Bull sick, we get a cab and go down into the slums to find El Indio (the Black Bastard he's called in the trade), who always has something—It's always been my secret hunch that El Indio loves Tristessa too—He has beautiful grown daughters, he lies in a bed behind flimsy curtains with the door wide open to the world, high on M, his elder wife sits anxiously in a chair, ikons burn, arguments take place, groans, all under the endless Mexican skies—We come to his pad and his old wife tells us she is his wife (we didnt know) and he's not in so we sit on the stone steps of the crazy courtyard full of screaming children and drunks and women with wash and banana peels you'd think, and wait there—Bull is so sick he has to go home—Tall, humped, wizard cadaver-like he goes, leaving me sitting drunk on the stone drawing pictures of the children in my little notebook—

Then out comes a host of some kind, a portly friendly man, with a waterglass of pulque, two glasses, he insists I chugalug mine with his, I do, bang, down, the cactus

juice dripping from our lips, he beats me to the draw—
Women laugh—There's a big kitchen—He brings me
more—I drink and draw the children—I offer money
for the pulque but they wont take it—It starts to grow
dark in the courtyard—

I've already swallowed a fifth of wine on the way down,
it's one of my drinking days, I've been bored and sad
and lost—too, for three days I've been painting and
drawing with pencil, chalk and watercolors (my first for-
mal try) and I'm exhausted—I've sketched a little
bearded Mexican artist in his roof hut and he tore the
picture out of the big notebook to keep it—We drank
tequila in the morning and drew each other—Of me he
drew a kind of tourist sketch showing how young and
handsome and American I am, I dont understand (he
wants me to buy it?)—Of him I draw a terrible apocalyptic black bearded face, also his body tinily twisted on
the edge of the couch, O heaven and posterity will judge
all this art, whatever it is—So I'm drawing one particular
little boy who wont stand still then I start drawing the
Virgin Madonna—

More fellows appear and they invite me into a big
room where a big white table is covered with pulque
cups and on the floor open urns of it—Amazing the
faces in there—I think "I'll have a good time and meanwhile I'm right on El Indio's doorstep and I'll catch him
for Bull when he comes home—and Tristessa'll come
too—"

Borracho, we drain big cups of cactus juice and there's
an old singer with guitar with his young disciple boy

with thick sensitive lips and a big fat hostess woman like
out of Rabelais and Rembrandt Middle Ages who sings—
The leader of this huge gang of fifteen appears to be
Pancho Villa at the table end, red clay face, perfectly
round and jocund, but Mexican owlish, with crazy eyes
(I think) and a wild red checked shirt and like always
ecstatically happy—But beside him other more sinister
lieutenants of some sort, to them I look downtable right
dead in the eye and toast and even ask "Que es la vida?
What is life?"—(to prove I'm philosophical and smart)—
Meanwhile a man in a blue suit and blue hat appears
the most friendly, he beckons me to the toilet for a
swaying talk over urine—He locks the door—His eyes
are sunken deep in pudgy battered W.C. Fields sockets—
"sockets" too clean a word—but a wicked pair of funny
eyes, also a hypnotist, I keep staring at him, I keep *liking*
him—I like him so much that when he takes my wallet
out and counts my money I laugh, I fiddle a little bit
trying to get it back, he holds off counting—Others are
trying to get in the toilet—"This is Mexico!" says he.
"We stay here if we like"—When he hands me back my
wallet I see my money's still in it but I swear on the Bible
on God on Buddha on all that was supposed to be holy,
in real life there was no more money in that wallet (wallet,
shwallet, just a leather foldcase for travelers checks)—
He leaves me *some* money because later I give twenty
pesos to a big fat guy and tell him to go out and get
some marijuana for the whole group—He too keeps
taking me to the toilet for earnest confabs, somehow my
dark glasses disappear—

Finally Blue Hat in front of everybody simply snatches my notebook out of my (Bull's) coat, like a joke, pencil and all, and slips it in his own coat and stares at me, wicked and funny—I really cant help laughing but then I do say "Come on, come on, give me back my poems" and I reach into his coat and he twists away, and I reach again and he wont—I turn to the most distinguished-looking man there, in fact the only one, who is sitting next to me, "Will you undertake the responsibility of getting my poems back."

He says he will, without understanding what I'm saying, but I drunkedly assume he will—Meanwhile in a blind dazzle of ecstasy I throw fifty pesos on the floor to prove something—Later I throw two pesos on the floor saying "It's for the music"—They end up feeding that to the two musicians but I'm too proud after reconsideration to start looking around for my 50 pesos too but you will see that this is just a case of wanting to be robbed, a strange kind of exultation and drunken power, "I dont care about money, I am the King of the world, I will lead your little revolutions myself"—This I begin to work on by making friends with Pancho Villa, and brother there's a lot of knocking of cups and arm-around-chugalugs down, and song—And by this time I'm too stupid to check my wallet but every cent is gone—I take great pride meanwhile in showing how I appreciate the music, I even drum on the table—Finally I go out with Fat Boy to talk in the toilet and as we're coming out here comes a strange woman up the steps, unearthly and pale, slow, majestic, neither young nor old, I cant help staring at her and even when I realize it's Tristessa I keep staring and wondering at this strange woman and it seems that she has come to save me but she's only coming for a shot from El Indio (who, by the way, had by now, on his own accord, gone to Bull's two miles away)—I leave the gay gang of thieves and follow my love.

She is wearing a long dirty dress and a shawl and her face is pale, little rings under the eyes, that thin patrician slowly hawked nose, those luscious lips, those sad eyes—and the music of her voice, the complaint of her song, when she talks in Spanish to others . . .

AH SACRISTI—the sad mutilated blue Madonna, is Tristessa, and for me to keep saying that I love her is a bleeding lie—She hates me and I hate her, make no bones about it—I hate her because she hates me, no other reason—She hates me because I dont know, I guess I was too pious last year—She keeps yelling "*I dunt care!*" and hits us over the head and goes out and sits on the curb in the street and doodles and sways—Nobody dares approach the woman with her head between her knees—Tonight though I can see she's alright, quiet, pale, walking straight, coming up the stone steps of the thieves—

El Indio aint in, we go down again—I had already twice visited El Indio's to check on him, not there, but

his brown daughter with the beautiful brown sad eyes
staring out into the night as I question her, "Non, non,"
is all she can say, she is staring at some fixed point in
the garbage of the sky, so all I do is stare at her eyes
and I have never seen such a girl—Her eyes seem to say
"I love my father even tho he takes narcoticas, but please
dont come here, leave him alone"—

Tristessa and I go down to the slippery garbage street
of dull brown cokestand lights and distant dim blue and
rose neons (like rubbed chalk crayon) of Santa Maria de
Redondas, where we hook up with poor bedraggled wild
looking Cruz and start off somewhere—

I have my arm around Tristessa's waist and walk sadly
with her—Tonight she doesnt hate me—Cruz always
liked me and still does—In the past year she has caused
poor old Bull every kind of trouble with her drunk she-
nanigans—O there's been pulque and vomiting in the
streets and groans under heaven, spattered angel wings
covered with the pale blue dirt of heaven—Angels in
hell, our wings huge in the dark, the three of us start
off, and from the Golden Eternal Heaven bends God
blessing us with his face which I can only describe as
being infinitely sorry (compassionate), that is, infinite
with understanding of suffering, the sight of that Face
would make you cry—I've seen it, in a vision, it will cancel
all in the end—No tears, just the lips, O I can show
you!—No woman could be that sad, God is like a man—
It's all a blank how we go up the street to some small
narrow dark street where two women are sitting with

steaming cauldrons of some kind, or steamcups, where we sit on wood crates, I with my head on Tristessa's shoulder, Cruz at my feet, and they give me a drink of hot punch—I look in my wallet, no more money, I tell Tristessa, she pays for the drinks, or talks, or runs the whole show, maybe she's the leader of the gang of thieves even—

The drinks dont help much, it's getting late, towards dawn, the chill of the high plateau gets into my little sleeveless shirt and loose sports coat and shino pants and I start shivering uncontrollably—Nothing helps, drink after drink, nothing helps—

Two young Mexican cats attracted by Tristessa come and stand there drinking and talking all night, both have mustaches, one of them is very short with a round baby face with pear-like cheeks—The other is taller, with wings of newspaper stuck somehow in his jacket to protect him from the cold—Cruz just stretches out right in the road in her topcoat and goes to sleep, head on the ground, on the stone—A cop arrests somebody at the head of the alley, we around the little candle flames and steampots watch without much interest—At one point Tristessa kisses me gently on the lips, the softest, just-touchingest kiss in the world—Aye, and I receive it with amazement—I've made up my mind to stay with her and sleep where she sleeps, even if she sleeps in a garbage can, in a stone cell with rats—But I keep shivering, no amount of wrapping in can do it, for a year now I've been spending every night in my sleeping bag and I'm

no longer inured to ordinary dawn chills of the earth—
At one point I fall right off the crate I occupy with
Tristessa, land in the sidewalk, stay there—Other times
I'm up haranguing long mysterious conversations with
the two cats—What on earth are they trying to say and
do?—Cruz sleeps in the street—

Her hair hangs out all black across the road, people
step over her.—It's the end.

Dawn comes gray.

PEOPLE START PASSING to go to work, soon the pale
light begins to reveal the incredible colors of Mexico,
the pale blue shawls of women, the deep purple shawls,
the lips of people faintly roseate in general aubeal blue—

"What we waiting for? Where we goin?" I'd kept
asking—

"I go get my shot," she says—gets me another hot
punch, which goes down shivering through me—One
of the ladies is asleep, the dealer with ladle is beginning
to get sore because apparently I've drank more than
Tristessa paid or the two cats or something—

Many people and carts pass—

"Vamonos," says Tristessa getting up, and we wake
up ragged Cruz and waver a minute standing, and go
off in the streets—

Now you can see to the ends of the streets, no more

garbanzo darkness, it's all pale blue churches and pale
people and pink shawls—We move along and come to
rubbly fields and cross and come to a settlement of adobe
huts—

It's a village in the city by itself—

We meet a woman and go into a room and I figure
we'll finally sleep in here but the two beds are loaded
with sleepers and wakers, we just stand there talking,
leave and go down the alley past waking-up doors—
Everybody curious to see the two ragged girls and the
raggedy man, stumbling like a slow team in the dawn—
The sun comes up orange over piles of red brick and
plaster dust somewhere, it's the wee North America of
my Indian Dreams but now I'm too gone to realize anything or understand, all I wanta do is sleep, next to
Tristessa—She in her skimpy pink dress, her little breast-
less body, her thin shanks, her beautiful thighs, but I'm
willing to just sleep but I'd like to hold her and stop
shivering under some vast dark brown Mexican Blanket
with Cruz too, on the other side, to chaperone, I just
wanta stop this insane wandering in the streets—

No soap, at the end of the village, in the final house,
beyond which is fields of dumps and distant Church tops
and the bleary city, we go in—

What a scene! I jump to rejoice to see a huge bed—
"We're coming to sleep here!"

But in the bed is a big fat woman with black hair, and
beside her some guy with a ski cap, both awake, and
simultaneously a brunette girl looking like some artist

gal beatnik gal in Greenwich Village comes in—Then
I see ten, maybe eight other people all milling around
in the corners with spoons and matches—One of them
is a typical junkey, that rugged tenderness, those rough
and suffering features covered with a gray sick slick, the
eyes certainly alert, the mouth alert, hat, suit, watch,
spoon, heroin, working swiftly at shots—Everybody is
shooting up—Tristessa is called by one of the men and
she rolls up her coat sleeve—Cruz too—The ski cap has
jumped out of bed and is doing the same—The Greenwich Village gal has somehow slipt into the bed, at the
foot, got her big sensuous body under the sheets from
the other end, and lies there, glad, on a pillow, watching—People come in and out from the village outdoors—
I expect to get a shot too and I say to one of the cats
"Poquito gote" which I imagine means little taste but
really means "little leak"—Leak indeed, I get nothing,
all my money's gone—

The activity is furious, interesting, human, I watch
truly amazed, stoned as I am I can see this must be the
biggest junk den in Latin America—What interesting
types!—Tristessa is talking a mile a minute—The be-
hatted junkey with rough and tender features, with little
sandy mustache and faintly blue eyes and high cheekbones, is a Mexican but looks just like any junkey in New
York—He wont give me a shot either—I just sit and
wait—At my feet I have a half full bottle of beer Tristessa
had bought me en route, which I'd cached in clothes,
now I sip it in front of all these junkies and that finishes

my chances—I keep a sharp eye on the bed expecting the fat lady to get up and leave, and the artist gal at her feet, but only the men hustle and dress and get out and finally we leave too—

"Where we goin?"

We walk outa there through a saddler's prompt line of crossed sword eyes of miux ow you know, the old gantlet line, of respectable bourgeois Mexicans in the morning, but nobody stops us, no cops, we stumble out and down a narrow dirt street and up to another door and inside a little old court where an old man is sweeping with a broom and inside you hear many voices—

He pleads with me with his eyes about something, like, "Dont start trouble," I make the sign "*Me* start trouble?" but he insists so I hesitate to go in but Tristessa and Cruz drag me confidently and I look back at the old man who has given his consent but is still pleading with his eyes— Great God, he knew!

The place is a kind of unofficial morning snort-bar, Cruz goes into dark noisy interiors and comes out with a kind of weak anisette in a waterglass and I taste—I dont want any particularly—I just stand against the dobe wall looking at the yellow light—Cruz looks absolutely crazy now, with high hairy bestial nostrils like in Orozco the women screaming in revolutions but nevertheless she manages to look dainty too—Besides she is a dainty little person, I mean her heart, all night long she has been very nice to me and she likes me—In fact she'd screamed in a drunk one time "Tristessa you're jealous because Yack wanted to marry me!"—and but she knows I love unlovable Tristessa—so she's sistered me and I liked it—some people have vibrations that come straight from the vibrating heart of the sun, unjaded . . .

But as we're standing there Tristessa suddenly says: "Yack" (me) "all night"—and she starts imitating my shiver in the all-night street, at first I laugh, sun's yellow hot now on my coat, but I feel alarmed to see her imitate my shiver with such convulsive earnestness and Cruz notices too and says "Stop Tristessa!" but she goes on, her eyes wild and white, shivering her thin body in the coat, her legs begin to crumple—I reach out laughing "Ah come on"—she gets more shivery and convulsive and suddenly (as I'm thinking "How can she love me making fun of me *seriously* like that") she starts to fall, which imitation is going too far, I try to grab her, she bends way down to the ground and hangs a minute (just like descriptions Bull had just given me of heroin addicts nodding down to their shoetops on Fifth Avenue in the 20's Era, way down till their head hung completely from the necks and there was nowhere to go but up or flat down on the head) and to my pain and crash Tristessa just bonks her skull and falls headlong on it right on the harsh stone and collapses.

"*Oh no Tristessa!*" I cry and grab her under the arms and twist her over and sit her in my haunches as I hunch against the wall—She is breathing heavily and suddenly I see blood all over her coat—

"She's dying," I think, "suddenly she's decided now

to die . . . This insane morning, this insane minute"—
And here's the old man with the pleading eyes still looking at me with his broom and men and women going
in for anisette stepping right over us (with gingerly unconcern but slowly, scarcely glancing down)—I put my
head to hers, cheek to cheek, and hold her tight, and
say "*Non non non non*" and what I mean is "Dont die"—
Cruz is on the ground with us on the other side, crying—
I hold Tristessa by her little ribs and pray—Blood now
trickles out of her nose and mouth—

No one's gonna move us outa that doorway—this I
swear—

I realize I'm there to refuse to let her die—

We get water, on my big red bandana, and mop her
a little—After whiles of convulsive shuddering suddenly
she becomes extremely calm and opens her eyes and
even looks up—She wont die—I feel it, she wont die,
not in my arms nor right now, but I feel too "She must
know that I refused and now she'll be expecting me to
show her something better than that—than death's eternal ecstasy"—O Golden Eternity, and as I know death
is best but "Non, I love you, dont die, dont leave me . . .
I love you too much"—"Because I love you isnt that
enough reason to try to live?"—O the gruesome destiny
of we human beings, each one of us will suddenly at
some terrible moment die and frighten all our lovers
and carrion the world—and crack the world—and all
the heroin addicts in all the yellow cities and sandy des-
erts cannot care—and they'll die too—

Tristessa now tries to get up, I raise her by little broken armpits, she leans, we adjust her coat, poor coat, we wipe off a little blood—Start off—Start off in the yellow Mexican morning, not dead—I let her walk by herself ahead of us, lead the Way, she does so through incredibly dirty staring streets full of dead dogs, past gawking children and old women and old men in dirty rags, out to a field of rocks, across that we stumble—Slowly—I can sense it now in her silence, "*This* is what you give me instead of death?"—I try to know what to give her instead—No such thing better than death—All I can do is stumble behind her, sometimes I briefly lead the way but I'm not much the figure of the man, The Man Who Leads The Way—But I know she is dying now, either from epilepsy or heart, shock, or goofball convulsion, and because of that no landlady is going to stop me from taking her home to my room on the roof and letting her sleep and rest under my open sleepbag, with Cruz and me both,— I tell her that, we get a cab and start to Bull's—We get off there, they wait in the cab as I knock on his window for the money for the cab—

"*You cant bring Cruz here!*" he yells. "Neither one of em!" He hands me the money, I pay the cab, the girls get out, and there's Bull's big sleepy face in the door saying "No No—the kitchen is full of women, they'll never let you through!"

"But she's dying! I've got to take care of her!"

I turn and I see both their coats, the back of their coats, have majestically Mexicanly womanly turned, with

immense dignity, streaks of dust and all street plaster
and all, together, the two ladies go down the sidewalk
slowly, the way Mexican women aye French Canadian
women go to church in the morning—There is something unalterable in the way both their coats have turned
on the women in the kitchen, on Bull's worried face, on
me—I run after them—Tristessa looks at me seriously'
"I go down to Indio for to get a shot" and in that way
that normal way she always says that, as if (I guess, I'm
a liar, watch out!) as if she means it and really wants to
go get that shot—

And I had said to her "I wanta sleep where you sleep
tonight" but fat chance of me getting into Indio's or even
herself, his wife hates her—They walk majestically, I
hesitate majestically, with majestic cowardice, fearing the
women in the kitchen who have barred Tristessa from
the house (for breaking everything in her goofball fits)
and barred her above all from passing through that
kitchen (the only way to my room) up narrow ivorytower
winding iron steps that shiver and shake—

"They'd never let you through!" yells Bull from the
door. "Let em go!"

One of the landladies is on the sidewalk, I'm too
ashamed and drunk to look her in the eye—

"But I'll tell them she's dying!"

"Come in here! Come in here!" yells Bull. I turn,
they've got their bus at the corner, she's gone—

Either she'll die in my arms or I'll hear about it—

What shroud was the reason why darkness and heaven

commingled to come and lay the mantle of sorrow on
the hearts of Bull, El Indio and me, who all three love
her and weep in our thoughts and know she will die—
Three men, from three different nations, in the yellow
morning of black shawls, what was the angelic demonic
power that devised this?—What's going to happen?

At night little Mexican cop whistles blow that all is
well, and all is all wrong, all is tragic,—I dont know what
to say.

I'm only waiting to see her again—

And only last year she'd stood in my room and said
"A friend is better than pesos, a friend that geev it to
you in the bed" when still she believed anyway we'd get
our tortured bellies together and get rid of some of the
pain—Now too late, too late—

In my room at night, the door open, I watch to see
her come in, as if she could get through that kitchen of
women—And for me to go looking for her in Mexico
Thieves' Market, that's I suppose what I'll have to do—

Liar! Liar! I'm a liar!

And supposing I go find her and she wants to hit me
over the head again, I know it's not her it's the goofballs—but where could I take her, and what would it
solve to sleep with her?—a softest kiss from pale-rosest
lips I did get, in the street, another one of those and I'm
gone—

My poems stolen, my money stolen, my Tristessa
dying, Mexican buses trying to run me down, grit in the
sky, agh, I never dreamed it could be this bad—

And she hates me—Why does she hate me?
Because I'm so smart

"AS SURE AS you're sittin there," Bull keeps saying since that morning, "Tristessa'll be back tapping on that window on the thirteenth for money for her connection"—

He wants her to come back—

El Indio comes over, in black hat, sad, manly, Mayan stern, preoccupied, "Where is Tristessa?" I ask, he says, hands out, "I dont know."

Her blood is on my pants like my conscience—

But she comes back sooner than we expect, on the night of the 9th—Right while we're sitting there talking about her—She taps on the window but not only that reaches in a crazy brown hand through the old hole (where El Indio's a month ago put his fist through in a rage over junkless), she grabs the great rosy curtains that Bull junkey-wise hangs from ceiling to sill, she shivers and shakes them and sweeps them aside and looks in and as if to see we're not sneaking morphine shots on her—The first thing she sees is my smiling turned face— It must of disgusted the hell out of her—"Bool—Bool—"

Bool hastily dresses to go out and talk to her in the bar across the street, she's not allowed in the house.

"Aw let her in"

"*I cant*"

We both go out, I first while he locks, and there confronted by my "great love" on the sidewalk in the dim evening lights all I can do is shuffle awhile and wait in the line of time—"How you?" I do say—

"Okay"

Her left side of face is one big dirty bandage with black caked blood, she has it hidden under her head-shawl, holds it draped there—

"Where that happen, with me?"

"No, after I leave you, *tree times* I fall"—She holds up three fingers—She's had three further convulsions—The cotton batting hangs down and there are long strip tails down to almost her chin—She would look awful if she wasnt holy Tristessa—

Bull comes out and slowly we go across the street to the bar, I run to her other side to gentleman her, O what an old sister I am—It's like Hong Kong, the poorest sampan maids and mothers of the river in Chinee slacks propelling with the Venetian steer-pole and no rice in the bowl, even they, in fact they especially have their pride and would put down an old sister like me and O their beautiful little cans in sleek shiney silk, O—their sad faces, high cheekbones, brown color, eyes, they look at me in the night, at all Johns in the night, it's their last resort—O I wish I could write!—Only a beautiful poem could do it!

How frail, beat, final, is Tristessa as we load her into the quiet hostile bar where Madame X sits counting her pesos in the back room, facing all, and lil mustachio'd

anxious bartender darts furtively to serve us, and I offer
Tristessa a chair that will hide her sad mutilated face
from Madame X but she refuses and sits any old way—
What a threesome in a bar usually reserved for Army
officers and Mex businessmen foaming their mustaches
at mugs of afternoon!—Tall bony frightening hump-
backed Bull (what do the Mexicans think of him?) with
his owlish glasses and his slow shaky but firm-going walk
and me the baggy-trousered gringo jerk with combed
hair and blood and paint on his jeans, and she, Tristessa,
wrapt in a purple shawl, skinny,—poor,—like a vendor
of loteria tickets in the street, like doom in Mexico—I
order a glass of beer to make it look good, Bull con-
descends to coffee, the waiter is nervous—

O headache, but there she is sitting next to me, I drink
her in—Occasionally she turns those purple eyes at me—
She is sick and wants a shot, Bull no got—But she will
now go get three gramos on the black market—I show
her the pictures I've been painting, of Bull in his chair
in purple celestial opium pajamas, of me and my first
wife ("Mi primera esposa," she makes no comment, her
eyes look briefly at each picture)—Finally when I show
her my painting "candle burning at night" she doesnt
even look—They're talking about junk—All the time I
feel like taking her in my arms and squeezing her,
squeezing that little frail unobtainable not-there body—

The shawls falls a little and her bandage shows in the
bar—miserable—I dont know what to do—I begin to get
mad—

Finally she's talking about her friend's husband who's put her out of the house that day by calling the cops (he a cop himself), "He call cops because I no give im my *body*" she says nastily—

Ah, so she thinks of her body as some prize she shant give away, to hell with her—I pivot in my feelings and brood—I look at her feelingless eyes—

Meanwhile Bull is warning her about goofballs and I remind her that her old ex-lover (now dead junkey) had told me too never to touch them—Suddenly I look at the wall and there are the pictures of the beautiful broads of the calendar (that Al Damlette had in his room in Frisco, one for each month, over tokay wine we used to revere them), I bring Tristessa's attention to them, she looks away, the bartender notices, I feel like a beast—

AND ALL THE previous ensalchichas and papas fritas of the year before, Ah Above, what you doin with your children?—You with your sad compassionate and nay-would-I-ever-say unbeautiful face, what you doin with your stolen children you stole from your mind to think a thought because you were bored or you were Mind—shouldna done it, Lord, Awakenerhood, shouldna played the suffering-and-dying game with the children in your own mind, shouldna slept, shoulda whistled for the music and danced, alone, on a cloud, yelling to the stars you made, God, but never shoulda thought up and topped up tippy top Toonerville tweaky little sorrowers like us, the children—Poor crying Bull—child, when's sick, and I cry too, and Tristessa who wont even let herself cry . . .

OH WHAT WAS the racket that backeted and smashed in raging might, to make this oil-puddle world?—

Because Tristessa needs my help but wont take it and I wont give—yet, supposing everybody in the world devoted himself to helping others all day long, because of a dream or a vision of the freedom of eternity, then wouldnt the world be a garden? A Garden of Arden, full of lovers and louts in clouds, young drinkers dreaming and boasting on clouds, gods—Still the god's'd'a fought? Devote themselves to gods-dont-fight and bang! Miss Goofball would ope her rosy lips and kiss in the World all day, and men would sleep—And there wouldnt be men or women, but just one sex, the original sex of the mind—But that day's so close I could snap my finger and it would show, what does *it* care? . . . About this recent little event called the world.

"I love Tristessa," nevertheless I have the gall to stay and say, to both of them—"I woulda told the landladies I love Tristessa—I can tell them she's sick—She needs help—She can come sleep in my room tonight"—

Bull is alarmed, his mouth opens—O the old cage, he

loves her!—You should see her puttering around the room cleaning up while he sits and cuts up his junk with a razorblade, or just sits saying "M-m-m-m-m-m-m-m" in long low groans that arent groans but his message and song, now I begin to realize Tristessa wants Bull to be her husband—

"I wanted Tristessa to be my third wife," I say later— "I didnt come to Mexico to be told what to do by old sisters? Right in front of the faculty, shooting?—Listen Bull and Tristessa, if Tristessa dont care then I dont care—" At this she looks at me, with surprised not-sur- prised round she-doesnt-care-eyes—"Give me a shot of morphine so I can think the way you do."

They promptly give me that, in the room later on, meanwhile I've been drinking mescal again—" All or nothing at all," says I to Bull, who repeats it—

"I'm not a whore," I add—And I also want to say "Tristessa is not a whore" but I dont want to bring up the subject—Meanwhile she changes completely with her shot, feels better, combs her hair to a beautiful black sheen, washes her blood, washes her whole face and hands in a soapy washtub like Long Jim Beaver up on the Cascades by his campfire—Swoosh—And she rubs the soap thoroughly in her ears and twists fingertips in there and makes squishy sounds, wow, washing, Charley didnt have a beard last night—She cowls her head again with the now-brushed shawl and turns to present us, in the lightbulbed high-ceiling room, a charming Spanish beauty with a little scar on her brow—The color of her face is really tan (she calls herself dark, "As Negra as *me?*") but in the lights that shine her face keeps changing, sometimes it is jet-brown almost black-blue (beautiful) with outlines of sheeny cheek and long sad mouth and the bump on her nose which is like Indian women in the morning in Nogales on a high dry hill, the women of the various guitar—The Castilian touch, though it may be only as Castilian as old Zacatecas it is fitting— She turns, neat, and I notice she *has* no body at all, it is utterly lost in a little skimpy dress, then I realize she never eats, "her body" (I think) "must be beautiful"— "beautiful little thing"—

But then Bull explains: "She dont want love—You put Grace Kelly in this chair, Muckymuck's morphine on that chair, Jack, I take the morphine, I no take the Grace Kelly."

"Yes," asserts Tristessa, "and me, I no awanta love."

I dont say nothin about love, like I dont start singing "Love is a completely endless thing, it's the April row when feelers reach for everything" and I dont sing "Embraceable You" like Frank Sinatra nor that "Towering Feeling" Vic Damone says "the touch of your hand upon my brow, the look in your eyes I see," wow, no, I dont disagree or agree with this pair of love-thieves, let em get married and get under—go under the sheets— go bateau'ing in Roma—Gallo—anywhere—me, I'm not going to marry Tristessa, Bull is—She putters around him endlessly, how strangely while I'm lying on the bed junk-high she comes over and cleans up the headboard

with her thighs practically in my face and I study them
and old Bull is watching out of the top of his glasses to
the side—Min n Bill n Mamie n Ike n Maroney Maroney
Izzy and Bizzy and Dizzy and Bessy Fall-me-my-closer
Martarky and Bee, O god their names, their names, I
want their names, Amie n Bill, not Amos n Andy, open
the mayor (my father did love them) open the crocus
the mokus in the closet (this Freudian sloop of the mind)
(O slip slop) (slap) this old guy that's always—Molly!—
Fibber M'Gee be jesus and Molly—Bull and Tristessa,
sitting there in the house all night, moaning over their
razor-blades and white junk and pieces of broken mirror
to act as the pan (the diamond sharp junk that cuts into
glass)—Quiet evenings at home—Clark Gable and Mona
Lisa—

Yet—"Hey, Tristessa I live with you and Bull pay" I
say finally—

"I dont care," she says, turning to me on the stool—
"It's awright with me."

"Wont you at least pay half of her rent?" asks Bull,
noting in his notebook figures he keeps all the time.
"Will you say yes or no."

"You can go see her when you want," he adds.

"No, I wanted to live with her."

"Well, you cant do that—you havent got the money."

But Tristessa keeps looking at me and I keep staring
at her, suddenly we love each other as Bull drones on
and I admire her openly and she shines openly—Earlier,
I'd grabbed her, when she said "You remember every-

thing the other night?"—"Yes"—"in the street, how you kiss me"—And I show her how she'd kissed me.

That little gentle brush of the lips on the lips, with just the slightest kiss, to indicate kiss—She'd shined on that one—She didnt care—

She had no money to take the cab home, no bus was running, we had no more money any of us (except money in the bloodbank) (money in the mudbank, Charley)—"Yes, I walk home."

"Three miles, two miles," I say, and there was that long walk through the rain I remembered—"You can come up there," pointing to my room on the roof, "I wont bother you, no te molesta."

"No te molesta" but I would leave her molest me—Old Bull is glancing over his glasses and paper, I've screwed everything up with the mama again, Oedipus Rex, I'll tear out my eyes in the morning—San Francisco, New York, Padici, Medu, Mantua or anywhere, I'm always the King sucker who was made out to be the positional son in woman and man relationships, Ahhyaaaaa—(Indian howl in the night, to campo-country sweet musica)—"King, bing, I'm always in the way for momma and poppa—When am I gonna be poppa?"

"NO TE MOLESTA," and too, for Bull, my poppa,—I said: "I'd have to be a junkey to live with Tristessa, and I cant be a junkey."

"Aint nobody knows junkies like another junkey."

I gulp to hear the truth, too—

"Besides, too, Tristessa is an oldtime junkey, like me, she no chicken—in junk—Junkies are very strange persons."

Then he would launch into a long story about the strange persons he's known, in Riker's Island, in Lexington, in New York, in Panama—in Mexico City, in Annapolis—In keeping with his strange history, which included opium dreams of strange tiered racks where girls are being fed opium through dreamy blue tubes, and similar strange episodes like all the innocent *faux pas* he'd made, tho always with an evil greed just before it, he'd thrown up at Annapolis after a binge, in the showers, and to conceal it from his officers he'd tried to wash it down with the hot water, with the result the smell permeated "all of Bradley Hall" and there was a beautiful poem written about it in the newspaper of the Navy Goats—He would launch into long stories but she was there and with her he just conducted routine junkey talk in baby Spanish, like, "You no go tomorrow good look like that."

"Yes, I clean my face now."

"It no look good—They take one look at you and they know you takin too many secanols"

"Yes, I go"

"I brush your coat—" Bull gets up and helps clean her things—

To me he says, "Them artists and writers, they dont

like to work—Dont believe in work" (as the year before,
as Tristessa and Cruz and I chatted gayly with the gaiety
I had last year, in the room, he's banging with a Mayan
stone statue about the size of a big fist trying to fix the
door he'd broken down the night before because he took
too many goofballs and went out of his room and
locked-clicked the padlock, key in the room and him in
his pajamas at One A M)—wow, I do gossippy—(So he'd
yelled at me "Come help me fix this door, I cant do this
by myself"—"Oh yes you can, I'm talking"—"You artists
are all lazy bums")

Now to prove I'm not like that I get up slowly, dizzy
from that shot of their love stuff, and get some water
in the tin pitcher to heat on the upturned ray-lamp so's
Tristessa can have hot water for her wound-wash—but
I hand him the pitcher because I cant go thru the hassel
of balancing it on the flimsy wires and anyway he's the
old master Old Wizard Old Water Witch Doctor who
can do it and wont let me try it—Then I get back on the
bed, prostrate—prostate gland too, as morphine takes
all the sex out of your parts and leaves it somewhere
else, in your gut—Some people are all guts and no
heart—I take heart—You shoot spades—You drink
clubs—You blast oranges—I take heart and bat—Two—
Three—Ten trillion million dizzying powder of stars
fermangitatin in the high blue Jack Shaft—prop—I dont
drown no buddies in oil—I got no guts to do it—Got
heart not to—But the sex, when the morphine is loosed
in your flesh, and slowly spreads, hot, and headies your

brain, the sex recedes into the gut, most junkies are thin, Bull and Tristessa are both bags of bones—

But O the grace of some bones, that milt a little flesh hang-on, like Tristessa, and makes a woman—And Old Bull, spite of his thin hawky body nobody, his gray hair is well slicked and his cheek is youthful and sometimes he looks positively pretty, and in fact Tristessa had finally one night decided to make it and he was there and they made it, good—I wanted some of that too, seein's how Bull didnt rise to the issue except once every twenty years or so—

But no, that's enough, hear no more, Min n Molly n Bill n Gregory Pegory Fibber McGoy, oy, I'd leave them be and go my own way—"Find me a Mimi in Paris, a Nicole, a sweet Tathagata Pure Pretty Piti"—Like poems spoke by old Italians in South American palm mud, flat, who wanta go back to Palabbrio, reggi, and stroll the beauteous bell-ringing girl-walking boulevard and drink aperitif with the coffee muggers of the card street—O movie—A movie by God, showing us him—him,—and us showing him,—him which is us—for how can there be two, not-one? Palmsunday me that, Bishop San Jose . . .

I'll go light candles to the Madonna, I'll paint the Madonna, and eat ice cream, benny and bread—"Dope and saltpork," as Bhikku Booboo said—I'll go to the South of Sicily in the winter, and paint memories of Arles—I'll buy a piano and Mozart me that—I'll write long sad tales about people in the legend of my life— This part is my part of the movie, let's hear yours